STRANDED WITH THE RESORT OWNER

ANGEL'S PEAK STEAMY INSTALOVE POWER DYNAMIC NOVELS

BOOK THREE

ELLIE MASTERS

MASTER OF ROMANTIC SUSPENSE

JEM PUBLISHING

Published in the United States of America

JEM Publishing

This is a work of fiction. While reference might be made to actual historical events or existing locations, the names, characters, businesses, places, and incidents are either the product of the author's imagination or are used fictitiously, and any resemblance to actual persons, living or dead, business establishments, events, or locales is entirely coincidental.

DEDICATION

This book is dedicated to my one and only—my amazing and wonderful husband.

Without your care and support, my writing would not have made it this far.

You pushed me when I needed to be pushed.

You supported me when I felt discouraged.

You believed in me when I didn't believe in myself.

If it weren't for you, this book never would have come to life.

ALSO BY ELLIE MASTERS

The LIGHTER SIDE

Ellie Masters is the lighter side of the Jet & Ellie Masters writing duo!
You will find Contemporary Romance, Military Romance,
Romantic Suspense, Billionaire Romance, and Rock Star Romance
in Ellie's Works.

YOU CAN FIND ELLIE'S BOOKS HERE:

ELLIEMASTERS.COM/BOOKS

SUGGESTED READING ORDER

START HERE

Rockstar Romance

The Angel Fire Rock Romance Series

EACH BOOK IN THIS SERIES CAN BE READ AS A STANDALONE
AND IS ABOUT A DIFFERENT COUPLE WITH AN HEA. IT IS
RECOMMENDED THEY ARE READ IN ORDER.

Heart's Insanity

Ashes to New

Heart's Desire

Heart's Collide

Hearts Divided

Hearts Entwined

Forest's FALL

Hearts The Last Beat

CONTINUE HERE...

By Jet & Ellie Masters

Ellie Masters writing as L.A. Warren

Vendel Rising: a Science Fiction Serialized Novel

If you enjoyed this book by Ellie Masters, the LIGHTER SIDE of the Jet & Ellie writing duo, and aren't afraid of edgier writing, you might enjoy reading BDSM themed books written by Jet, the DARKER SIDE of the Masters' Writing Team.

The DARKER SIDE

Jet Masters is the darker side of the Jet & Ellie writing duo!

Romantic Suspense

Changing Roles Series:

THIS SERIES MUST BE READ IN ORDER.

Command Me

Control Me

Collar Me

Embracing FATE

Seizing FATE

Accepting FATE

HOT READS

A STANDALONE NOVEL.

Down the Rabbit Hole

Light BDSM Romance

The Ties that Bind

EACH BOOK IN THIS SERIES CAN BE READ AS A STANDALONE AND IS ABOUT A DIFFERENT COUPLE WITH AN HEA.

Alexa

Penny

Michelle

Ivy

HOT READS

Becoming His Series

Dark Captive Romance

To My Readers

This book is a work of fiction. It does not exist in the real world and should not be construed as reality. As in most romantic fiction, I've taken liberties. I've compressed the romance into a sliver of time. I've allowed these characters to develop strong bonds of trust over a matter of days.

This does not happen in real life where you, my amazing readers, live. Take more time in your romance and learn who you're giving a piece of your heart to. I urge you to move with caution. Always protect yourself.

BLURB

When perfectionist event coordinator Amelia Hayes arrives at The Haven at Angel's Peak, she's ready to execute the high-profile wedding that could launch her career—until a blizzard traps her alone with the resort's infuriatingly attractive owner.

Lucas Cross left his cutthroat corporate past behind to restore his family's mountain resort. The last thing he needs is a control-freak planner storming into his quiet sanctuary... or the undeniable attraction that ignites the moment they crash into each other—literally—on the icy steps.

With the wedding staff snowed out and the power down, Amelia and Lucas are forced to share his remote cabin—complete with one bed, no backup, and a rising heat that has nothing to do with the fire. As their forced proximity turns to something deeper, they'll have to confront what matters more: keeping control... or letting love in.

But when the snow clears and real life closes in, will their connection melt away—or spark something permanent?

Tropes You'll Love:
 Forced Proximity
🔥 One Bed
💼 Grumpy/Sunshine
🪓 Opposites Attract
📝 Workaholic Heroine
🤍 Reclusive, Protective Hero

- 💋 Dominant Dirty Talk
- 🎯 High-Stakes Career vs. Love

CHAPTER 1

PERFECT PLANS INTERRUPTED

THE SNOW FALLS IN DELICATE, LAZY SPIRALS AS I navigate the winding mountain road up to the small town of Angel's Peak. My knuckles turn white against the steering wheel as my grip tightens. Each curve brings The Haven at Angel's Peak closer, and with it, the culmination of six months of obsessive planning. My checklist cycles through my mind on an endless loop: centerpieces, seating arrangements, backup generators for the outdoor lighting.

Everything must be flawless.

Executed to perfection.

The resort materializes through the curtain of snowflakes, a sprawling timber and stone structure that commands the mountainside. Light glows from windows like beacons against the darkening afternoon sky. The view steals my breath, just as it did in the glossy brochures I showed the Mortons when convincing them this remote location was worth the extravagant price tag.

I park near the entrance, gathering my leather portfolio and the color-coded binder that has become my third arm since landing the Morton-Wells wedding. Charlene Morton—

daughter of tech billionaire Richard Morton—deserves nothing less than perfection, and I intend to deliver exactly that.

The memory of my last conversation with Miranda, my razor-sharp boss at Elite Events, surfaces unbidden.

"This isn't just any wedding, Amelia." She leaned across her immaculate glass desk, red fingernails tapping an ominous rhythm. "This is the social event of the season—of the decade. Every detail will be scrutinized by people who can make or break careers—yours and mine. Don't disappoint me."

The weight of that responsibility settles deeper into my shoulders as I step from the car, the cold air slicing through my wool coat. The Mortons and two hundred of their closest friends and business associates arrive in four days. Everything must be ready.

I adjust my grip on the binder and portfolio, tightening my scarf against the biting wind. The snowfall has intensified during the drive, no longer picturesque flurries but determined flakes with purpose and weight. My boots connect with the first of the wide stone steps leading to the grand timber entrance, and I mentally rehearse my opening speech to the resort staff.

That's when gravity betrays me.

My foot slides on an invisible patch of ice. My arms pinwheel in a desperate bid for balance, sending my precious binder flying. The world tilts sideways, and I brace for impact.

It never comes.

Strong hands grip my elbows, steadying me against a solid chest. Heat radiates through my coat, a stark contrast to the frigid air whipping around us.

"Easy there." The voice above me holds a hint of amusement. "The mountain doesn't surrender her secrets to those in a hurry."

I push away, regaining my footing and my dignity in one

movement. My rescuer stands before me, tall and broad-shoul-dered with dark hair dusted in snowflakes. His eyes crinkle at the corners, deep blue and entirely too self-satisfied.

"My binder!" I scan the steps frantically, spotting pages and tabs scattered across the snow like colorful confetti. The leather organizer lies half-buried in a snowdrift, its contents spilling out in a disastrous rainbow. "No, no, no!"

I lunge for the nearest pages, nearly slipping again. Dropping to my knees, I frantically grab at color-coded tabs and meticulously organized schedules before the wind can carry them away. Six months of work disintegrating in the snow.

"You're welcome." The man crosses his arms, amusement deepening the lines around his eyes. "Most people say thank you after being saved from a concussion."

"Most people would help pick up these papers instead of standing there smirking." I snatch at a floating seating chart, my fingers numb with cold and panic. The wind mocks me, lifting another sheet just as I reach for it.

He sighs, then kneels beside me, gathering pages with efficient movements. "We're not expecting any guests today."

"I'm not a guest." I snatch a page from his hand, shoving it haphazardly into the binder. My perfectly organized system is now complete and utter chaos. "I'm Amelia Hayes, event coordinator for the Morton-Wells wedding."

Recognition flickers across his features, followed by something that looks suspiciously like dismay. It vanishes quickly, replaced by an easy smile that transforms his face, softening the sharp angles of his jaw and cheekbones.

"Lucas Reid." He extends a hand, still holding several of my rescued papers. "Owner and manager of The Haven at Angel's Peak."

The revelation hits like a splash of icy water. This is the man I've exchanged countless emails with over the past six months? The meticulous resort owner who assured me every detail would be addressed with the utmost care?

His hand remains extended. I shift my binder and grasp it briefly, noting calluses that seem out of place for a luxury resort owner. His palm radiates warmth against my cold fingers.

"Let's get you inside before you turn into an overly organized icicle." He reaches for my portfolio, but I clutch it closer.

"I can manage."

"Suit yourself." He shrugs and moves toward the heavy wooden doors, holding one open. "After you, Ms. Hayes."

The resort lobby unfolds before me, a soaring space of exposed beams and stone. A massive fireplace dominates one wall, flames leaping behind an ornate iron screen. The scent of pine and woodsmoke wraps around me, momentarily soothing my jangled nerves.

But only momentarily.

The lobby should be bustling with staff preparing for the wedding. Instead, it stands eerily quiet. No reception staff. No event team. Just vast, empty luxury.

"Where is everyone?" I turn to Lucas, dread building in my stomach.

"It's just me tonight." He shrugs, setting my partially rescued papers on a solid wooden console table. "The staff will be here first thing tomorrow."

"Just you?" My voice rises despite my efforts to maintain professionalism. "I mean your staff. The event team that should be transforming the reception hall according to the schedule I sent three weeks ago. The florists who should be preparing arrangements for the rehearsal dinner. The—"

"They'll be here first thing tomorrow." He moves toward the fireplace, seemingly unconcerned by my rising panic. "Most of them live in town, and there's no need for them to stay overnight when we don't have guests yet."

"No need?" My voice cracks with strain. "Mr. Reid, I specifically outlined in my communications that preparations needed to begin today. The Mortons are arriving in four days, and everything must be perfect when they walk through that door."

He turns, the firelight casting shadows across his face. "And it will be. My team knows what they're doing."

"Your team isn't here." I gesture to the empty lobby, my carefully constructed schedule crumbling before my eyes. "I need to inspect the reception hall, finalize the table arrangements, check the lighting and sound systems—"

"All of which can be done tomorrow morning." His calm only fuels my anxiety. "We've hosted hundreds of events, Ms. Hayes. Trust me, everything will be ready."

Trust. Such a simple word, yet impossible to extend to this man with his relaxed posture and casual dismissal of my concerns. I've built my career on meticulous planning and personal oversight, not blind faith in strangers.

"I need to see the reception hall." I move toward the corridor that should lead to the main event space, according to the floor plans I've memorized.

Lucas sighs but follows. "Fine. But I promise, you'll find it exactly as we discussed."

The grand ballroom doors swing open to reveal a cavernous space with floor-to-ceiling windows that would showcase mountain views if not for the snow now pelting against the glass. The room stands empty save for stacked chairs and folded tables along one wall.

My heart sinks. "This doesn't look 'exactly as we discussed' to me, Mr. Reid."

"Lucas." He corrects automatically. "And yes, it needs to be set up. Which will happen tomorrow morning when my team arrives."

I open my binder, flipping through the scattered remains

of my detailed timeline. "According to this schedule, which you approved, we should be starting setup today, with gradual progress over the next three days before the guests arrive."

"Plans change." He shrugs, seemingly impervious to my distress. "The weather forecast shifted. I told the staff to come in early tomorrow instead of staying late tonight."

As if summoned by his words, the lights flicker once, twice, then stabilize. Lucas frowns, glancing toward the ceiling.

"Let's head back to the lobby." He gestures toward the door. "I want to check something."

We return to the grand entrance, where Lucas walks to a large television mounted above the fireplace. It displays a weather map covered in swirling white and blue. A meteorologist gestures emphatically at the storm system engulfing the entire mountain range.

"—unexpected intensity has prompted officials to close Highway 14, the only access road to Angel's Peak and surrounding areas. Residents and visitors are advised to shelter in place until further notice. We're looking at accumulations of up to three feet in the next twenty-four hours, with high winds creating whiteout conditions—"

The room tilts beneath my feet. "The road is closed? But I need your staff here to begin preparations. We have a strict schedule to keep if we're going to be ready for the wedding."

"The snow didn't get that memo." Lucas's expression has finally lost its casual confidence.

I gesture toward the windows, where flakes now drive horizontally against the glass. "What are we going to do?"

He runs a hand through his hair, disheveling the dark strands. "First, we stay calm. Weather in the mountains is unpredictable. The road will likely reopen tomorrow once the plows get through."

The lights flicker again, longer this time, before plunging

us into complete darkness. The only illumination comes from the crackling fire and the ghostly reflection of snow against the windows.

"Perfect. Just perfect." My voice sounds distant to my own ears, shock numbing my usual problem-solving abilities.

"Don't worry." Lucas's silhouette moves toward a control panel near the wall. "The generator will kick in any second."

We wait. Nothing happens except the increasing howl of wind rattling the massive windows.

"Or not." He sighs. "The backup system should have started automatically."

"And if it doesn't?" The cold already seeps into the room as the fire provides the only heat.

"Then we adapt." His gaze locks with mine, firelight dancing in those blue depths. "That's what you do as an event planner, right? Adapt when things don't go according to plan?"

The question hits uncomfortably close to home. My reputation at Elite Events stems from my ability to execute flawless events exactly as planned—because I leave nothing to chance. Adaptation has never factored into my professional vocabulary.

"I prevent problems before they occur." The words sound hollow even to me. "I don't leave things to chance."

"Well, Ms. Hayes." He gestures toward the howling storm beyond the windows. "I don't think either of us planned for this."

My phone buzzes in my pocket—a lifeline to the outside world. I fumble it out with shaking fingers, Miranda's name flashing on the screen.

"Please tell me you've arrived and everything is on schedule." Her voice cuts through the static of the poor connection.

I turn away from Lucas, lowering my voice. "I've arrived, but we have a situation. There's a storm, and it's intensifying. They've closed the only road in, and now the power's out."

"They've what?" Her voice rises sharply. "That's unacceptable. We have a strict timeline. Do you understand what's at stake here?"

"Of course I do, but—"

"No buts. Find a solution. That's what I pay you for." The connection crackles. "I'm losing signal. Call me when you've fixed this."

The line goes dead, leaving me staring at the screen. Fix this? As if I can command the weather to bend to my will.

"Bad news?" Lucas's voice startles me in the darkness.

I slip the phone back into my pocket, squaring my shoulders. "Nothing I can't handle. I need to make some calls and see what I can salvage of this disaster."

He moves toward the fireplace, adding another log. The flames leap higher, casting dancing shadows across the room. "I'm going to check the generator. The controls are outside. Stay here where it's warm."

"What about all the rooms?" I wrap my arms around myself, already feeling the chill creeping in as heat escapes through the soaring ceiling.

Lucas pauses at the heavy entrance door, snow gusting in as he cracks it open. "Without power, none of the rooms will have heat. The fireplaces are our only option right now."

The door closes behind him with a heavy thud, leaving me with the crackling fire and my flawless plans unraveling. I pull my coat tighter, watching snowflakes batter against the windows like tiny fists demanding entry.

Ten minutes pass before the door reopens, admitting a gust of freezing air and a snow-covered Lucas. His cheeks are reddened from the cold, his dark hair dusted white.

"The generator is completely buried in snow." He brushes

ice crystals from his shoulders. "And something's wrong with the backup system. I can't fix it in this storm."

"So what do we do?" I ask, approaching the fire for warmth.

"We have two options." He shrugs off his coat, snow-dusted and heavy, hanging it on the hook near the door.

I should be focused on logistics—weather alerts, backup power, guests, emergency protocols.

Instead, I'm hyper-aware of every movement he makes. The way his sweater pulls across broad shoulders and muscular chest. How his jeans ride low on narrow hips. How snowflakes melt in his hair and slide down his neck. How he rolls up his sleeves with slow, capable hands.

Good God.

His forearms are corded with muscle, dusted with dark hair, veins visible beneath golden skin. Functional strength, not the kind sculpted in a gym—earned by physical work. What is wrong with me?

"I can keep the fire going all night if we stay here in the main lodge." His voice is low, unhurried, with just enough rasp to make my pulse skip. "But it's a big space to heat."

He crosses the room, each step echoing in the vast space. My throat tightens. The scent of pine and firewood trails after him, and something warm and wrong pulses deep in my belly.

I force my eyes to stay on his face. Not his mouth. Not his hands.

"And the other option?" I manage, though my voice comes out thinner than I'd like.

He turns, face shadowed with firelight, eyes steady on mine. "My private lodge. Just behind the main building. Smaller. More efficient. Has its own generator and fireplace."

"That sounds like the better choice," I say too quickly.

He doesn't move. Doesn't smile. Just watches me with that maddening calm. "It only has one bed."

Oh no.

Heat flares low in my stomach, spreading like wildfire. My brain dives straight into dangerous, utterly inappropriate territory.

I imagine that bed—him in it, shirtless, sheets tangled around his hips. Me on my knees. His voice dark and rough, telling me what to do. Yeah, I have particular tastes when it comes to sex.

Jesus, Amelia.

And then, because my brain is clearly trying to destroy me tonight, the fantasy sharpens. His hands, precise and commanding. That calm voice explaining exactly how I'll beg for release—and when I'll get it.

If this unfairly gorgeous man knows how to take control—

I'd be done. Absolutely, irreversibly wrecked.

I snap my attention back to his face, to the faint scar at the edge of his brow, the steady weight of his gaze. My pulse stutters like it's trying to tap out a warning.

I am so fucked.

The storm has hijacked my schedule, my event, and now my sanity.

I'm about to spend the night in a cabin—one bed, one man—with someone who looks like sin, smells like cedar, and probably knows exactly how to undo a woman with a single word. I check his left hand. No wedding ring.

He's available, and I'm thinking very inappropriate thoughts.

My thoughts spiral—rough hands, heat between my thighs, his mouth everywhere.

Completely inappropriate.

Absolutely uncontrollable.

Dangerous.

I draw a breath. Force a smile.

Remain professional, Amelia.

"It's small, intimate, but comfortable," he adds, voice dry. Amused.

The words snap through the fog like a slap.

I blink. Realize I've been staring—openly, shamelessly—at his hands. His chest. His mouth.

Goddamn it.

Heat floods my cheeks. I tear my gaze away, pretending to find the floorboards fascinating.

When I risk a glance back up, he's still watching me— brows slightly raised, mouth curved at the corners. Not smug. Not mocking. Just... knowing. Like he saw every single place my mind wandered.

My stomach flips.

He knows.

He definitely knows.

I picture him above me. Not just in that bed—but owning it. Hands braced beside my head, his body pinning mine, that mouth rough and hungry. The kind of kiss that leaves bruises. His hips thrusting deep, punishing. The kind of dominating sex that ruins women.

Criminal and forbidden.

So far past inappropriate, it should be illegal.

I blink hard, trying to scrub the image from my brain, but it's already branded there. Permanent.

My self-control is officially circling the drain because the last thing I need is a man like him—built like a threat, quiet like a storm—occupying my thoughts.

I stare at him. Broad shoulders. Scarred knuckles. That slow, unreadable gaze. I square my shoulders, trying to salvage what's left of my dignity.

"Well?" Lucas raises an eyebrow, waiting for my response.

"Lead the way."

His smile deepens—just a fraction. My thighs clench, and

my thoughts remain firmly in dangerously unprofessional territory.

The real risk tonight isn't the blizzard.

It's him—and all the things I shouldn't want him to do to me.

I'm not afraid of the cold. I'm scared of what will happen when he closes that cabin door behind us.

Chapter 2

Heat Index

Lucas leads me through the lodge in silence, our footsteps echoing softly across polished wood floors. The distant crackle of the fire fades behind us as we reach the back door. He pushes it open, holding it for me, and the sound of the wind surges in like a living thing.

We step under the covered walkway, and everything narrows. The world is white and shadowed, the edges of the structure crusted with snowdrifts that creep in beneath the slats. Wind whistles through the cracks, sharp and relentless, but in here it's just the sound of his boots against weathered planks—and the pounding rhythm of my pulse.

The walk to his lodge is short, but it feels like miles. Snow whips around us, cold needles against my cheeks, but the heat under my skin makes it bearable. Or maybe it's adrenaline.

Each step drives home just how alone we are out here.

Cut off.

Sealed in.

I tell myself it's just the cold. Just exhaustion.

Just survival.

But the heat beneath my skin says otherwise.

I focus on the rhythm of his footsteps in front of me. He walks ahead, his pace unhurried, every movement precise. Controlled. That kind of effortless strength that comes from a man who never second-guesses himself.

It shouldn't be hot. But it is.

He glances back once, and our eyes catch in the dim light. No words. No smile. Just heat.

Not imagined.

Not one-sided.

Just there—undeniable.

My stomach dips. My breath catches. I follow him, heart thudding, every nerve wound tight.

His private lodge looms ahead, smaller than the main building but still impressive—modern lines, warm cedar, and windows that gleam with reflected firelight. He unlocks the door and pushes it open, gesturing me inside.

Our gazes lock and simmer.

Warmth hits me like a blanket. The fireplace is already lit, casting golden light over thick wooden beams and worn leather furniture. The space is cozy—almost too intimate. Like the kind of place you bring someone when you want to blur lines.

There's a sleek kitchen tucked into one corner, the countertops gleaming in the firelight. A spiral staircase winds up toward a lofted area, open and shadowed, while the main floor remains dominated by one thing: the bed.

A king-sized, four-poster bed.

Flannel sheets, thick comforter, pillows stacked like he's expecting someone to stay. The posts are thick—dark wood, polished smooth—and at the top, just beneath the crossbeams... rings.

I blink. Look again.

Definitely rings. Metal. Anchored into the frame.

There's no door to the bedroom. Just a wide, square opening that leads straight into the sleeping area like a dare. The ceilings stretch high above, and my eyes lift instinctively—catching on something else.

Hooks. Bolted into the beam overhead.

Oh my God.

My brain is spinning before I can stop it. Those rings at the top of the bed... the hooks in the ceiling... restraints?

I'm probably imagining it. I have to be imagining it. Right?

But the moment the thought enters my mind, it stays—taking root, unfurling into a vivid, inappropriate fantasy I can't unsee. Ropes. Wrists bound above my head. His hands on my hips, his mouth on my skin, that voice—deep and steady—telling me I'm not allowed to come until he says so.

Heat floods low in my belly, sharp and instant.

I swallow hard, eyes dragging back to the bed like it's trying to tell me a story my body already knows by heart.

I am in so much trouble.

It's perfect.

Too perfect.

He shuts the door behind us. The lock clicks.

My pulse spikes.

"This is it," he says, voice low and smooth, like he's welcoming me into something more than just shelter. "It's not much, but it keeps the cold out."

Lucas tosses his gloves onto the entry table with a quiet thud. Then he unbuttons his flannel jacket, slow and unhurried, like this is just another night—like he brings strange women into his private lodge all the time and never thinks twice.

He drapes the jacket over a chair and straightens, revealing the fit of the dark sweater beneath. It clings to his torso, outlining thick shoulders and a chest built for carrying weight —literal and otherwise.

My fingers twitch. My brain screams don't stare, but that's a battle I'm already losing.

"Living room, kitchen," he says with a nod, gesturing like he's giving me a tour of a hotel suite. "Bathroom's through there. My bed." His voice dips slightly on the last word, rough around the edges.

He meets my eyes when he speaks again. "Blankets are in the chest. I'll take the couch."

I turn in a slow circle, trying not to visibly short-circuit. The whole place smells like pine, woodsmoke, and him—clean and masculine with a sharp, underlying edge that makes my skin prickle. A scent that should be bottled and weaponized.

"You don't have to," I say, too fast. "It's your bed."

I try to make it sound casual. Light. Like I'm unaffected. I'm not.

He shrugs, that same maddening half-smile playing at the corner of his mouth. "I insist." A beat. "Like I said... the couch is comfortable."

His eyes flick to mine, deliberate. And there's something in his tone—something too smooth to be innocent.

My gaze drops because I can't look at him when he says things like that. Not when my brain is still running slow-motion reels of the bedposts and ceiling hooks. I focus on the couch. The tiny, insufficient, going-to-fold-him-in-half couch.

Right. Comfortable. Sure.

"Right," I murmur. "Well. This is... cozy."

He chuckles, low and quiet, as he moves toward the fire-place. Stokes it with the kind of ease that says he doesn't need to fill silences with noise.

"This is temporary," he says, still not looking at me as he

stokes the fire. "Just tonight. In the morning, I'll fix the main generator. Get you back to the lodge."

Back to normal. Back to safe.

"And if the storm doesn't let up?" I ask, my voice softer now. Less sure.

He glances over his shoulder, firelight carving shadows along his cheekbone, his mouth curved just slightly—like he already knows the effect he's having.

"Then you're stuck here," he says, tone low and unhurried. "Trapped in my cabin. With me."

A pause. A flicker of heat in his eyes.

"Could be worse."

Silence stretches between us. Heavy. Loaded.

I force myself to move, walking to the fireplace with arms crossed tight across my chest like that'll hold in the storm building under my skin. My thoughts are spiraling again— rope, rough hands, control, surrender. The same reel, playing louder now. Closer.

He watches me. Says nothing.

But I feel his eyes on me.

I rub my arms—not from cold, but to ground myself against the buzz crawling along my nerves. It doesn't help.

Lucas moves past me, crouching at the hearth. He stokes the fire with casual precision that makes everything worse. Each movement is quiet and deliberate, and his body language is easy—like he's in control of the room, the fire, and me.

His broad shoulders shift beneath that damn sweater. His sleeves are still pushed up, revealing forearms that should come with a warning label—tan skin, corded muscle, thick ropey veins that disappear under the edge of his cuff.

I should be setting boundaries. Making a plan. Saying something smart and responsible.

Instead, I say, "So... are you always this prepared for

weather-related emergencies, or is this your subtle way of luring unsuspecting women into your lair?"

He straightens, slow and fluid, and when he turns to face me, his expression strips the air from my lungs. His eyes are darker now. Focused. Heat curling in their depths like he's already undressing me in his head—and maybe retying me in something else.

"Only the ones who look like they need it," he says, voice low, intimate. "Or want it."

My stomach flips.

My thighs clench.

The silence between us thickens, buzzing with the things we're both pretending we're not thinking. I force myself to breathe. To blink. Don't look down.

I fail.

My eyes flick to his hips—and yep.

There it is.

His jeans are tight. Too tight. Straining just enough to make my mouth go dry and my brain short-circuit.

I drag my gaze back up, slowly, like I'm afraid of what else I'll see.

He doesn't look smug. Doesn't look cocky.

He just looks.

At me.

Like he's deciding.

I should move. Walk away. Unpack. Build a pillow fort of professional distance.

But I don't. I just stand there, heat crawling up my neck, my pulse hammering in my throat.

Lucas takes a single step toward me.

I don't retreat.

Another step.

Close enough now that I can see the flecks of silver in his eyes, the taut set of his jaw, the muscle ticking as he holds himself back. The firelight flickers across his face, and for a second, he looks like something carved from heat and control and hunger.

He watches me with that unreadable gaze—but now it's fraying at the edges. Tight. Coiled. Ready to snap.

"Amelia," he says, voice low and rough. "If you keep standing there looking at me like that..."

My breath hitches. "Like what?"

His eyes drop to my mouth. Linger. His voice is smoke and sin. "Like you want me to pin you against the nearest wall and give you everything you've been fantasizing about since the lodge."

I go still. Completely still. The words land like a match dropped in gasoline.

The air thickens, charged with the same electricity that lives in the seconds before thunder.

He steps closer—slow, deliberate—until we're toe to toe, chest to chest, heat to heat.

"I'm not blind," he murmurs. "And, fair warning, I sure as hell ain't a saint."

My lungs forget how to work. My blood pounds everywhere at once. I can smell him—smoke and pine and that scent I haven't stopped thinking about since he first opened the damn lodge door.

"I'm not trying to make this weird," I whisper, even though it already is. My voice trembles, not from fear, but anticipation. "We're two professionals. Adults. Stranded in a blizzard. We can survive one night in close quarters without it turning into—"

"Into what you've been imagining since you saw my bed?"

His mouth is right at my ear now, the heat of his breath dragging across my neck like a promise.

The heat in my cheeks explodes into something darker.

Deeper. My core tightens like it's responding to his voice alone.

"You've been looking at me," he growls, "like you want me to tie you to that bed and ruin you."

My lips part. I can barely breathe, but I manage the only thing I have left.

"You're not wrong."

Chapter 3

Three Choices, One Ruin

Chapter 3: Three Choices, One Ruin

His eyes flare. Not surprised. Not smug. Just... released. The last thread of control snapping clean.

"And here I've been trying to be a gentleman," he says.

The words hit me like a punch—low, sharp, hot.

"What now?" I whisper.

"Now, I'm wondering why I'm even pretending."

He closes the distance, and the air between us ignites. His fingers brush along my jaw, calloused and warm, tipping my face up like I already belong to him. His other hand slides to my waist, gripping firmly, dragging me against the full heat of his body.

He's hard. Solid. There.

The contact shoots through me like lightning.

His lips hover a breath above mine, his voice nothing but gravel and fire.

"This doesn't have to mean anything beyond tonight..."

A pause.

"But I promise you, if you let me take charge—it'll be everything you've imagined."

Then his hand fists in my hair, and his mouth crashes into mine—devouring, dominant, utterly unapologetic.

I don't answer. I can't.

Because he's already taken control—of my mouth, my breath, my body, my sanity.

It's instant combustion.

The kiss is brutal in its honesty—no hesitation, no sweet pretense. Just heat and hunger and all the filthy, forbidden things I've been aching for since the moment I laid eyes on him.

His hands slide to my waist, and in one swift movement, my back hits the wall with a thud that echoes through me. His body presses in, hips grinding, thigh wedged between mine, dragging a moan from somewhere deep.

I grind against him instinctively, shameless, chasing friction. His growl rumbles against my lips—low, primal, devastating.

He grips my thighs, lifts me effortlessly. I wrap around him without thinking, my skirt riding high, breath ragged. His mouth claims mine again—hot, wet, punishing—his tongue sliding against mine making my core clench.

Then his lips are at my jaw, trailing down my neck, his teeth grazing that sensitive spot that sends a pulse straight to my spine. "You smell like sin," he murmurs, voice wrecked. "And I've had enough of pretending I don't want you."

My fingers find the hem of his sweater, yanking it up, desperate to get to skin. I drag my nails along the ridges of muscle beneath and feel him shudder. He curses—raw and filthy—as he sets me down just long enough to strip the sweater off and toss it aside.

And then he's on me again.

His mouth. His hands. The fire he's lighting under my skin.

He grabs my thighs again, and this time when he lifts me,

there's no pause. No hesitation. Just claiming. One hand drags my dress up, baring me completely. His palm slides up the inside of my thigh, and I gasp—already soaked, already ready.

His other hand moves between us. I hear the low rasp of his zipper. His mouth is still on mine, devouring every breath.

Then his voice—low, dangerous—right against my lips.

"Tell me to stop."

My eyes snap open. He's close enough to see every flicker of restraint in his expression, like he's balancing on the edge of something feral.

"I'm not going to do that," I whisper, barely able to speak around the thudding of my pulse.

His eyes darken. His mouth curves—not soft, not sweet.

Predatory.

"Good."

He growls and lifts me again, this time without hesitation. One hand slides beneath my dress, fingers gliding through slick heat that confirms every unspoken thing between us.

"Fuck," he mutters. "You're soaked for me already."

I can't speak. Can't breathe.

My back hits the wall. My legs lock around his waist. And in one brutal thrust, he's inside me—deep, stretching me open, making me his.

My gasp is swallowed by his mouth. His tongue takes over, claiming everything, leaving no part of me untouched.

Then he starts to move.

Hard. Fast. Relentless.

A man on a mission.

Rutting. Fucking.

He pounds into me, each thrust slamming me against the wall, making me feel every inch, every ruthless intention in his body.

"You like this?" he growls against my neck, his voice pure gravel. "Like me fucking you senseless?"

I moan—helpless, wrecked.

"Yeah, you do. You love it. Love being pinned up like this. Nowhere to go. Nothing to do but take it."

Each word is punctuated by a thrust—hard, filthy, devastating.

"Wrapped around me... trembling like this... fuck, you were made for this. For me."

I cry out as his hand fists in my hair, tugging just enough to arch my neck and expose more of my throat. His teeth scrape across my skin. I'm already burning for him.

"Look at you," he growls, fucking me harder. "So fucking tight. So desperate. You love this—love being held like you're helpless while I fuck you against the goddamn wall."

My hands claw at his shoulders, nails digging into muscle. My moans break into gasps with every thrust.

He's relentless. Savage. Perfect.

My orgasm builds fast, blinding. Pressure twisting, heat tightening, nerves snapping.

"I can feel you," he growls. "About to come. I should make you beg for it, but I'm feeling generous."

I shatter at his filthy words.

My scream rips into his mouth as I convulse around him, body clenching so hard it nearly breaks me. Pleasure rips through me—raw, full-body, white-hot.

"Fuck," he snarls, hips jerking. "Take it. Take all of it."

He slams in deep, one last time, and goes still—groaning my name against my skin as he spills inside me, his entire body shuddering.

Silence crashes in.

Breathless. Shaky. Just the fire and the brutal thud of our hearts.

He doesn't move. Just leans his forehead to mine, both of us drenched in heat and sweat and something that feels too much.

Eventually, he sets me down, slow and careful. His hands linger like he's not quite ready to let me go.

I tug my dress down over my trembling thighs, still pulsing from the aftershocks.

"I'll get some water," he says, like he didn't just completely unmake me.

He walks away like he didn't just fuck me into the wall.

Casual. Loose. Zipper undone. His cock—still half-hard, slick and heavy—swings between his thighs as he moves.

I can't stop staring.

He strides into the kitchen, muscles flexing beneath that bare torso like a fucking predator—wolfish, unapologetic. He opens the fridge, grabs a bottle of water, cracks it, and takes a slow pull. His throat works, muscles rippling with every swallow.

Then he looks at me.

That look burns. Pure heat. Pure hunger.

"You okay?" he asks, voice deceptively mild. "Not what you expected when you came up here, I'm guessing."

I don't answer. Can't. My legs are trembling, my panties ruined, and he's standing there like he's got all the time in the world to do it again.

He sets the bottle down and starts walking back—slow, deliberate. His cock bounces slightly with every step, thick and tempting and not done.

He stops in front of me. Lifts a brow.

"I've been thinking about fucking you since I caught you on the stairs," he says, voice rough. "That tight little skirt. That mouth. The way you tried to pretend I didn't get under your skin."

He turns and gestures toward the bed.

Four-poster. Rings gleaming in the firelight.

Then he points up.

Ceiling beam. Hooks.

I swallow.

"You have three choices," he says, voice like sin. "You pick... or I'll pick for you."

He steps closer. His cock brushes against my dress. Deliberate.

"One—" he lifts a finger, "I tie you to that bed and make you scream so loud you lose your voice. Wrists bound. Legs spread. Nothing but my mouth and cock and your begging."

He leans in, lips just shy of mine.

"Two—" another finger lifts, "you drop to your knees and suck me like you've been fantasizing about since the lodge. You have been fantasizing about it... haven't you, Amelia?"

I suck in a breath, but he doesn't let me answer.

"Three," he says, smile curling wicked and slow, "you tell me I'm in charge and I decide which one comes first."

He steps back half a pace. Just enough to give me space. But his eyes never leave mine.

"You've got three seconds." His voice drops to a growl. "Choose."

My mouth is dry. My legs, still trembling. Every part of me throbs—from the stretch of him, the impact of his words, the promise of what he wants next.

Three choices.

All of them filthy. All of them perfect.

I meet his gaze—steady, smoldering—and find the strength I didn't know I still had.

"I choose all three."

His brows lift. His smile? Predatory.

But I'm already moving.

I drop to my knees on the soft rug in front of him, lifting my chin as I stare up at him, lips parted, voice low and shaking but sure.

"This one first."

His cock twitches. His hand fists at his side.

"Fuuuuck," he growls, voice thick. "You have no idea what that just did to me."

I wrap my fingers around the base of his cock, already hardening again in my hand, thick and heavy, hot against my palm.

He watches me—completely still, like a beast stalking prey —until I lick a slow, deliberate stripe along the underside of him.

He hisses through his teeth. "Shit. Just like that."

My tongue circles the tip, gathering the taste of him. My lips part, and I take him into my mouth, slow at first, savoring the weight of him, the way he fills me.

"God, you look good like that," he mutters, voice wrecked. "On your knees. Lips stretched around my cock."

I hum around him, and his hand snaps into my hair, not pulling—guiding. Just enough pressure to remind me who's really in control.

"You wanted this," he grits out. "You wanted to feel me on your tongue. Wanted to taste me, suck me, serve me."

I moan in response, cheeks hollowing as I slide deeper, saliva pooling, eyes watering as I take as much as I can.

"Fuck, Amelia—messy little mouth," he growls, thrusting shallowly into my throat. "You like it filthy, don't you? Like gagging on my cock while I praise you for being my good girl."

Heat rushes between my thighs. I grind against nothing, desperate and aching.

He drags me back, lets me breathe, just long enough to catch his eye. His pupils are blown, jaw tight, chest heaving.

Then he's back inside—thrusting deeper, harder.

"You're not getting off until I come down your throat," he growls. "And when I'm done, I'm tying you to that fucking bed and making you scream."

Tears sting my eyes, spit drips down my chin, and still I take him—faster, wetter, needier.

And when he explodes, it's with a grunt, hips jerking as hot release fills my mouth. I swallow instinctively, not even thinking—just obedient, wrecked, his.

He looks down at me, chest heaving, cock still twitching in my hand.

"Bed," he says, voice dark and final. "Now."

My legs barely work, but I rise—still trembling, lips swollen, his taste thick on my tongue.

He follows.

Slow. Controlled. Like he already knows exactly what he's going to do to me—and he's savoring every second before he makes good on every filthy word he's promised.

I back toward the bed, heart pounding, thighs slick. My dress is still bunched around my hips, everything about me wrecked and wanting.

He doesn't tell me to fix it.

Instead, he stops a few feet away, eyes dragging over every inch of me.

"Take it off," he says. Quiet. Commanding. Like fact.

I freeze.

Not because I don't want to obey.

Because the way he says it makes my knees weak.

His voice drops lower. "All of it."

My breath catches. Heat floods between my legs.

I reach for the zipper, hands shaking. Slide the dress down my body inch by inch, watching the hunger build in his eyes as each new strip of skin is revealed.

Bra next. Then panties.

By the time I'm bare, standing at the foot of his bed, I can feel the weight of his gaze like a touch.

He steps forward, one hand grazing my hip, the other curling around my wrist.

"Now," he murmurs, "lie back. Arms up."

He pulls rope from the chest at the foot of the bed—like it was already waiting. Like he knew this would happen.

He probably did.

He binds me fast, wrists secured to the rings at the headboard. The rope is smooth, tight, perfect—like he's done this before. Like he's an expert at tying up women and pulling every last scream from their throats.

"You have no idea what you've asked for," he murmurs, working the knots precisely, like a man about to destroy a thing he treasures.

The rope bites deliciously into my wrists, bound tight above my head. My legs are spread, restrained against the posts. I'm completely exposed. Helpless.

And he hasn't even touched me yet.

Lucas starts slowly.

Not gentle. Not hurried.

He teases. Nips. Licks.

"Already dripping," he murmurs against the inside of my thigh. "And I haven't even told you to beg yet."

Then he does. His tongue. His fingers. The low rasp of his voice commanding me to say what I want, to own it.

"You like being tied up like this?" His thumb circles my clit —barely there, maddening. "Like being spread for me... knowing you can't stop me?"

I writhe. Arch. Moan.

"Say it," he demands, voice low and lethal.

"Yes," I gasp. "God, yes."

He smiles against me. "Good girl."

He doesn't stop.

He brings me right to the edge—twice—then backs off, cruel and precise.

"Lucas—please—"

"Please what?" he asks, fingers dragging through the slick

heat between my thighs. "Please make you come? Please fuck you? Please wreck you?"

"Yes," I sob. "All of it."

And then he ruins me.

His mouth. His fingers. His cock.

He fucks me like he has a point to prove—no mercy, no filter, no pause.

I beg. I writhe. I come until I'm sobbing. And still, he keeps going.

He climbs over me—his body a wall of heat, muscles tense, cock thick and hard against my thigh.

"You wanted this," he growls in my ear. "Wanted to know what it feels like to be fucked until you forget your name."

Then he thrusts into me in one savage stroke—and I scream.

His hand grips my chin, tilting my face toward his. His eyes are dark, pupils blown wide with hunger and power.

"Tell me you want this," he growls, voice low and deadly. His hips roll once—slow, cruel—grinding against my slick core, just enough to make me gasp. "Tell me you want to please me. To be mine. Is that what you want?"

I can't speak. Can barely breathe.

His grip tightens, thumb brushing over my lips. "Say it."

My pulse pounds in my ears, heat surging everywhere at once. I feel like I'm going to explode if I don't answer him. If I don't give in.

"Yes," I whisper.

He leans in closer. "Louder."

"Yes," I gasp, voice shaking. "I want it—I want all of it."

His groan is feral.

"Good girl."

And then he drives into me—one brutal, claiming thrust —and I'm lost.

He fucks me like he's etching his name inside me. Every

thrust deep, brutal, perfect. He says things I don't even remember later—filthy, filthy promises—while he breaks me apart.

"Look at you," he pants, sweat dripping down his temple. "So fucking wet. So full of me. Your body's begging, even when your mouth can't speak."

And he's right.

I beg. I writhe. I come again—shaking, sobbing, ruined.

My voice breaks.

My thoughts scatter.

All that's left is him—his voice, his hands, his cock.

He keeps going.

Until I'm limp.

Until I'm empty.

Until the only word I know is Lucas.

When it's over, I'm shaking in the aftermath—thighs quivering, wrists still bound, breath broken. My entire body aches in the best, worst way.

Lucas lies beside me, propped on one elbow, watching me, heat still simmering low in his gaze.

He doesn't speak. Doesn't have to.

I've never felt more claimed.

And I know he's not finished.

Not even close.

But for now...

He unties my wrists, movements gentle. His fingers trail down the marks the rope left behind, like he's memorizing what he made.

He pulls me into his arms, settles me against his chest, his hand stroking my hair as I drift into the deepest, darkest, sweetest kind of ruin.

And in his bed, tangled in heat and sweat and the wreckage of what we just did...

I sleep like I've never slept before.

Chapter 4

Control Issues

Sunlight streams through the cabin's windows, painting golden patterns across the rumpled sheets. I stretch languidly, every muscle in my body gloriously sore. Memories of last night flood back in vivid detail—strong hands pinning my wrists above my head, hot breath against my neck, whispered commands that made me shiver with desire. My body still hums with the aftershocks of pleasure so intense I forgot my own name.

Who would have thought the laid-back resort owner could be so... commanding? So attuned to exactly what I needed before I even knew myself?

The space beside me is empty, though the sheets still hold his warmth. I roll onto my stomach, burying my face in his pillow to inhale the intoxicating scent of pine and musk. A smile curls my lips as I recall how thoroughly he dismantled every wall I'd built, how completely I surrendered control to him.

The aroma of fresh coffee pulls me from the haze of sleep and soreness. I blink against the light, reluctant to leave the warm nest of blankets and the vague ache between my thighs that reminds me exactly why I'm sore in the first place.

Lucas's shirt—thick flannel, abandoned in a frenzy last night—lies crumpled nearby. I slip it on. It falls to mid-thigh, sleeves dangling past my fingertips, smelling like cedar and sex and him.

Lucas stands at the stove in the kitchen, flipping pancakes like he didn't absolutely wreck me against the bedposts six hours ago. His back is to me—broad shoulders, jeans slung low on his hips, the waistband slightly askew like he tugged them on in a hurry. He's barefoot, humming to himself, steam rising from a French press beside him.

Unbothered. Unapologetic.

Completely at ease in the aftermath of a night that left me half-feral and mostly incoherent.

"Good morning." My voice is huskier than intended, still raw from hours of begging and gasping and screaming his name.

He turns, those penetrating blue eyes sweeping over me in a slow appraisal that makes heat bloom across my skin. A knowing smile plays at the corners of his mouth.

"Morning." He flips another pancake without looking. "Sleep well?"

"Not much." I attempt a casual tone that doesn't quite land. "Someone kept me busy."

His laugh is low and sensual, stirring embers I thought thoroughly extinguished. "No complaints were registered at the time." He pours a mug of coffee and hands it to me.

"None whatsoever." I grab the coffee, grateful for something to anchor me. The mug's still warm, the brew strong and black. Exactly how I need it.

I take a sip. He watches me over his shoulder.

"You moaned louder than the wind last night," he says casually. "Might've scared off the storm."

Heat floods my cheeks. I roll my eyes and will my body not to react to the memory of his mouth on me. Again. And again.

"We need to talk about the wedding."

His expression shifts, the playful lover retreating behind the mask of the relaxed resort owner. "Before breakfast?"

"We've lost a day already, and with the storm projected to last another three, that puts us dangerously close to—"

"A wedding that's still four days away." He slides a plate of pancakes across the counter. "Everything will get done, Amelia."

His tone is maddeningly relaxed. Infuriating. Like the whole world can pause while he makes pancakes and plans his next round of sex.

I try to focus on the pancakes. Not on how he moves. Not on how good his arms look flexing when he flips a pancake. Not on the way his jeans hang just low enough that I can see the dip of muscle leading—

"You don't understand." The pancakes look delicious, but anxiety has already begun its familiar crawl up my spine. "Even if the roads clear tomorrow, we've lost critical setup time. The florists need to begin arrangements, and the lighting crew needs to install the custom fixtures, the—"

He cuts me off, stepping closer, coffee mug still in hand like we're chatting about the weather.

"And all of that will still be there," he says, voice low and maddeningly calm, "after pancakes... after I bend you over the counter... and after shower sex."

My mouth opens. Closes. Nothing comes out.

"You're impossible," I manage, barely keeping my voice even.

He takes a sip of coffee, then nods toward the plate he made me. "Either eat your pancakes..." He leans in close, lips grazing the shell of my ear. "Or bend over."

My knees threaten to give out. My nipples pebble beneath his shirt. And he knows it.

Our eyes lock across the counter. Part of me—the part still buzzing from his touch—wants to yield. The other part—the professional event planner responsible for a multi-million-dollar wedding—cannot.

"I need to make a list at least." I reach for my phone, abandoned on the counter last night, when his kisses rendered technology irrelevant.

Lucas sighs, sliding a fork beside my plate. "You don't know how to stop, do you?"

The words sting more than they should. "Some of us can't afford to be so... relaxed."

"Is that what you think I am? Relaxed?" Something dangerous flashes in his eyes. "You, of all people, should know better after last night."

Heat floods my cheeks as images from our encounter flash through my mind—the controlled power in his movements, the meticulous attention to every detail of my pleasure, the unwavering focus that left me breathless.

The cabin's lights flicker once, twice, then stabilize. Lucas glances toward the ceiling, frowning.

"Generator's struggling in the cold." He moves toward the window, peering out at the accumulated snow. "If it fails, we'll need to move back to the main building and rough it by the fireplace."

"Another complication." I push my barely-touched breakfast aside, anxiety superseding hunger. "We should check the resort. Make sure there's no damage from the storm."

Lucas regards me silently for a long moment, then nods. "Finish your coffee, at least. I'll get dressed."

He disappears into the bedroom, leaving me alone with my racing thoughts and cooling pancakes. The spell of last night feels increasingly distant as reality reasserts itself.

What was I thinking, falling into bed with a man whose relaxed approach to business directly threatens my career? One night of mind-blowing sex doesn't change the fundamental conflict between us.

And yet, my body still tingles with the ghost of his touch. The memory of his voice, rough with desire, whispering exactly what he planned to do to me...

I shake my head, forcing my attention to the storm outside. The snow has stopped for now, though the accumulation looks significant. Drifts pile against the cabin's windows, transforming the world into a crystalline fortress of white.

Beautiful, but isolating.

Much like the connection we shared last night—intense but temporary, a product of extraordinary circumstances and steamy chemistry rather than any real compatibility.

Lucas returns dressed in jeans and a thick sweater, hair still damp from a quick shower. He tosses me a bundle of clothing.

"These will be too big, but they're warm. The path to the main building is covered, but the snow's deep."

I retreat to the bathroom to change, grateful for the moment alone to compose myself. The woman in the mirror looks different somehow—cheeks flushed, lips slightly swollen, eyes bright with lingering satisfaction.

I barely recognize her.

Dressed in his borrowed clothing—jeans rolled at the ankles, sweater slipping off one shoulder—I emerge to find Lucas by the door, pulling on heavy boots.

"Ready?" He holds out a thick parka. His expression is neutral.

He watches me cross the room, his eyes scanning over the oversized clothes hanging off my body—his clothes. And for the first time since waking, the easy confidence he's worn like a second skin... falters.

"You didn't finish your breakfast," he says, voice cool.

"Wasn't hungry." I tug the sweater's hem down self-consciously. "Too much on my mind."

"Right. The wedding." His jaw tightens. Something in his tone makes me glance at him, really look. He's not smiling. His gaze is distant. Shielded. "Guess I read the room wrong."

"It's not that," I start, then stop. Because it is that. At least partly.

Last night was mind-shattering, yes. But this morning? We're back to reality, and reality looks like a checklist with too many moving parts and a man who flips pancakes while casually threatening to tie me up again.

I reach for the parka, but he doesn't let go.

"I didn't expect flowers and promises, Amelia." His gaze meets mine, steady. "But I also didn't expect you to pretend last night didn't happen."

"It's not that." I stiffen.

The words come too fast. Too sharp.

Because if I don't say them fast, I'll start thinking about what last night actually was.

Not a hookup. Not a release.

It was... everything I crave but never ask for.

The edge I always chase.

Not sweetness. Not softness.

Control.

Total surrender.

And not the kind dressed up with safe words and candlelight.

No—real domination. No mercy. No pause.

No holding back.

He did things to me I've never let anyone do.

Because no one's ever been able to take it that far without making it feel fake.

Until him.

Last night was the closest I've ever come to being completely undone... and feeling safe in the ruin.

But I can't say that. Not to him. Not when I know this means something very different to him than it does to me. Or maybe that's just what I want to believe.

He doesn't flinch. Doesn't blink.

"Last night was... nice."

"Nice?" His voice drops. "You jump into bed with strangers all the time, then? Let them tie you up, fuck you until you sob, fall asleep wearing their shirt?"

My breath catches. My lips part.

I can't speak.

He steps closer—not threatening. Just there. Solid. Unshakable. Heat radiating off him like the fire we never finished last night.

"There's scratching an itch," he says, softer now. "And then there's what happened last night. What you let me do to you... It was more than... *nice*."

"I'm sorry. I'm just focused on my to-do list."

His eyes lock on mine. "Are you really going to stand there and tell me last night meant nothing?"

I shove my arms into the parka, fingers fumbling at the sleeves, the guilt hitting sharp under my ribs.

"It was chemistry, Lucas. Intense, overwhelming, and insanely hot chemistry. But that's all."

His smile is tight. Clipped. "Casual as mind-blowing sex can be between two very... compatible people."

"Exactly."

He studies me for a beat, then shakes his head like he sees through every carefully rehearsed line.

"I think the only thing we can agree on here," he mutters, "is that's a lie."

CHAPTER 5

RUINED BY THE TRUTH

LUCAS OPENS THE DOOR, LETTING IN A BLAST OF frigid air, and walks out without another word.

I follow him out into the snow, boots crunching behind his. The covered path to the main lodge is half-buried, the world around us gleaming and silent.

But it's not just the cold that has me shivering.

Because I keep thinking about the way he touched me. The way he looked at me. Like he saw more than a body to ruin—like he wanted to know the shape of my surrender and maybe even the why behind it.

And I can't stop hearing his voice from last night.

You wanted to be claimed. Made to obey. Made to please.

It shouldn't mean anything.

It doesn't.

Except...

Maybe it does.

And that's what terrifies me.

The resort's main building looms ahead—dark, cold, and

quiet under a fresh coat of snow. We crunch through drifts along the covered walkway, the silence between us louder than the wind.

Lucas says nothing.

He moves like a man already thinking five steps ahead—no teasing, no lingering looks, no trace of the man who whispered filth in my ear while I was tied to his bedpost last night.

Just... practical, focused daytime Lucas.

He pulls a heavy ring of keys from his pocket and slides one into the service entrance lock without hesitation.

"We'll need to check for pipe damage first." His breath fogs in the frigid air, white clouds spilling past lips that kissed every inch of my body twelve hours ago. "If any have burst, we could have serious water damage."

His voice is level. Crisp. Not cold, exactly—but distant.

Like he's flipped a switch.

Like last night is already filed away in a box labeled irrelevant.

And somehow, that hurts more than anything he said this morning.

I fall into step beside him as he pushes open the door. The air inside is even colder, the echo of our footsteps bouncing off empty walls.

Lucas reaches for a breaker panel. Flips switches. Checks valves. His attention never strays. His expression never cracks.

He's a man at work.

Professional. Capable. Completely in control.

Like I didn't fall apart under him last night.

Like I didn't sob his name into his pillow.

Like I'm not standing here now, still aching from how thoroughly he broke me open.

He glances back once. Just to check the light overhead.

Not me.

Not anymore.

We head to the lobby next, which feels cavernous without electricity. Shadows pool in corners the gray daylight can't quite touch. Our footsteps echo across the marble floor, and the space is eerily quiet except for the occasional groan of settling beams.

Lucas leads the way, expression neutral, steps purposeful.

"This way." He gestures toward a side hallway. "Maintenance panel's back here."

His voice is easy. Light. But it's not the same voice that growled against my throat. It's not the one that coaxed confessions from my lips while his fingers pushed me past the edge.

It's his business voice.

Professional. Detached. Warm enough to be polite and cool enough to remind me we're no longer tangled up in bedsheets.

"My grandfather built this place in the sixties." He kneels before a panel and flips a few switches. "It was just a small lodge then. Ten rooms, a shared dining space. No plumbing in half the units."

He glances over his shoulder, a faint smile appearing. "Pretty sure he'd have a stroke if he saw the spa additions."

I nod, because what else can I do?

He turns back to the panel, testing pressure valves and jotting notes onto a pad he pulls from his back pocket. All competent efficiency. No tension. No awareness of the fact that I'm still wearing thermal leggings over bare skin that's bruised and tender from the way he held me last night.

I fold my arms, trying not to fidget. Trying not to feel.

Because this is who he really is, right? The resort owner. The man with old keys and a legacy to protect. Not the one who bent me over and whispered how good I looked when I begged.

And me? I'm just the event planner. One night in a blizzard doesn't change that.

"You've expanded it considerably." I run my fingers over the rich wooden paneling lining the hall, letting the texture distract me from the ache in my chest.

"He left it to me five years ago." Lucas's voice softens, threaded with something almost nostalgic. "I'd just quit my corporate job—burnout, classic case. Eighty-hour weeks, constant travel, and relationships that couldn't survive my schedule. I was a mess."

The quiet honesty in his tone catches me off guard. It's not teasing. Not flirtatious. Just... real.

"What did you do before?" I ask, more softly than intended.

"Acquisitions and restructuring for ZentCorp." He moves toward another panel, checking gauges. "I specialized in hospitality properties. Buying struggling hotels, streamlining operations, flipping them for profit."

The information jolts me. "You were a corporate raider?"

"I preferred 'efficiency expert.'" His smile holds no humor. "I was very good at cutting costs and maximizing shareholder value."

"That doesn't align with..." I gesture vaguely around us.

"The laid-back mountain man?" His laugh is self-deprecating. "That's the point. This place—caring for something instead of dismantling it—saved me."

He glances over at me, then, expression unreadable. "Hard to know what you want when you're pretending nothing matters."

The words hit low. Direct. And not entirely about him.

I swallow, pulse flickering in my throat.

He's not looking at me anymore. He's already walking ahead, stepping around a drift of snow that's crept inside the building.

And that's when it hits me.

He's doing exactly what I said I wanted. Professional. Polite. Emotionally detached. No mixed signals. No flirtation.

No follow-up to the things he did to me with his mouth, his hands, and his voice.

And somehow... it's worse than if he teased me. Worse than if he made a joke or thrown a smug look my way.

Because now, I'm the one who wants more.

And he's the one pretending last night didn't mean anything.

Exactly like I told him to.

We move deeper into the resort, checking rooms for damage. The contrast between the man before me and the corporate shark he describes is difficult to reconcile—yet it explains the surprising control he exhibited in bed, the precision with which he'd taken me apart and put me back together.

It also explains his need to overwhelm and dominate completely.

And damn, if he doesn't do a bang-up job of that.

"Let's check the upper floors." Lucas gestures toward the elevator. "It's on a separate backup system—should still have power."

I follow him into the ornate elevator, its brass fixtures gleaming faintly even in the ambient gray light. The doors close behind us with a soft hush, sealing us inside.

Lucas presses the button for the top floor.

For a moment, nothing happens.

Then the elevator shudders softly and begins to rise— smooth and slow, the hum of machinery vibrating faintly beneath our feet.

Neither of us speaks.

The space feels tight. Too quiet. Every second stretched thin between us.

We're halfway up when the elevator lurches—hard.

The lights flicker once, twice—

And then everything goes black.

Only the dim emergency light above the control panel remains, casting a weak amber glow across the confined space. Shadows stretch across Lucas's face, sharpening the angles of his jaw and making his expression unreadable.

He exhales slowly and then checks the panel. Presses the button again. Nothing.

"Well, that's not ideal." He mutters, reaching into his back pocket for his phone. He flips it over, the screen lighting up his face briefly—cool blue against warm shadow. "No signal, of course."

"So we're stuck?" I ask, trying to keep my voice level. The silence between us is louder than ever now. Thicker.

"For now." His voice is calm. Controlled.

But he's not looking at the panel anymore. He's looking at me.

And the space suddenly feels a whole lot smaller.

"Now what?" My voice lands too loud in the tight space, brittle and sharp like glass cracking under pressure.

Lucas steps closer, heat radiating from him in the cold air.

"Now, we wait."

"For how long?" The air feels heavy. The silence is thick with everything we're not saying. Every memory of his hands on my body. His mouth on my skin.

He shrugs, voice low. "Until someone finds us. Or the power kicks back in."

He leans in—just enough for the shadows to swallow his features—and murmurs near my ear, "Could be a while. And I can think of several ways to keep warm."

I let out a short, dry laugh. "Is that all you can think about?" I lean back against the wall, arms folded. "I spread my legs for you once, and now you think it's an all-you-can-eat buffet?"

He stills.

The silence that follows isn't empty. It's loaded. Dense with heat. Tension. Threat.

His head tilts slightly. "Is that what you think I'm doing? Helping myself to another serving?"

His voice isn't angry. It's quiet. Intentional. Dangerous.

Then he steps closer—invading my space, swallowing the air between us in a single breath. His body radiates heat, dominance, control.

And something inside me... flips.

Just like that.

My knees nearly give. My breath catches. Every nerve ending snaps to attention like a good little soldier waiting for orders.

It's the power in his eyes. The deliberate way he waits for my answer like he already knows I don't have one. The way he looms without ever lifting a hand—commanding with nothing but presence.

And it wrecks me.

Because this is what I crave. This feeling. The primal, feral need to drop to my knees and give him everything. No hesitation. No safe words. No pretending.

Just him. Taking. Owning. Mastering.

"What are you afraid of?" He braces one arm against the wall beside my head, dragging his gaze over me like a promise I'm not ready for. "Is it me?"

He leans in, his mouth a breath from mine, voice molten.

"Or is it the fact that the only time you really feel anything... is when you're being fucked like it doesn't mean a thing?"

And god help me—I moan.

Inside, everything keens.

Because he's not wrong, and we both know it.

I inhale sharply. My spine straightens. "That's not—"

"No?" He leans in, mouth brushing my cheek as he speaks. "Because that's what you said this morning. That it meant nothing. And you meant it, didn't you?"

I don't answer. I can't.

His fingers graze my jaw, slow. Purposeful.

"Maybe that's the only way you can take it. Hard. Aggressive. Detached." His lips ghost across my ear. "You want it impersonal? You want it to feel like you're just a body?"

I should move. I should stop this.

But my knees are already going weak.

"You like it when it's rough because then you don't have to feel. You don't have to want. You just take."

My silence is answer enough.

Something shifts.

His hand wraps around my throat—not choking, just holding. Claiming.

"You want impersonal?" His voice is low, brutal.

I swallow hard. Nod once.

His hand tightens—just slightly—reminding me who's in control.

"Then I'm going to give it to you." He growls, voice molten steel. "Exactly how you say you want it. No sweet nothings. No gentle touches. Just you taking what I give."

He launches himself at me, closing the distance in a breath, hand gripping my throat—not tight, just firm, enough to make my pulse stutter under his grip.

His mouth crashes down on mine—hot, dominant, claiming. One hand still on my throat, the other yanking the sweater up and over my head in a single rough motion. The cold air hits my skin like a slap, but then he's everywhere—mouth on my neck, teeth scraping my collarbone, hands sliding down to cup my ass.

The air charges—static, electric—as he spins me without warning, pressing me hard against the elevator wall. My palms slap the cold metal, my breath catching in my throat as his body cages mine from behind.

I feel his cock, hard and ready, grinding against me through denim.

"You don't want it to mean anything?" His voice is a snarl in my ear. "Let's play pretend."

He shoves my leggings down, fast and rough. I gasp as cold air hits my thighs, followed by the sharp heat of his palm sliding between my legs.

"This is what control feels like." He hooks his fingers in the band of my panties and rips—rips—them down, the sound shockingly loud in the confined space. "You'll take it because I say so. Because I want it and because you need it. Because every part of you is begging to be ruined."

My forehead hits the wall. My mouth parts in a moan I can't contain.

"You're fucking wet." He mutters. "You want this, even now. Especially now. You've been asking for this since the moment you challenged me." He pushes my legs wider with his knee. "And now, I'm going to give it to you—rough, filthy, and exactly the way you like it. I'm going to fuck you." He growls against my lips. "And it's going to hurt."

I gasp, but he doesn't stop.

"It's going to hurt." He continues. "Because that's what I want. And you?" His palm flattens on my chest, holding me in place. "You're just a body I'm going to take from."

His words slap harder than his hands ever could.

But I don't stop him.

I don't stop him because he's right. Not that I could.

He doesn't wait. Doesn't ask again.

He enters in one brutal thrust, no warning, no softness. Just the stretch and burn of being filled fast and deep.

I cry out, body jerking, hands scrambling for purchase on the smooth surface.

Each movement is punishing. Unapologetic. He fucks me like I'm not a person, but a need. Something he has to consume. Own. Like this is about him now—his hunger, his dominance, his right to take.

"Yeah." He growls behind me. "That's what you wanted, right? Hard. Fast. Nothing personal. Just a cock and a hole."

My nails scrape the elevator wall. My teeth sink into my lip. I nod, gasping, sobbing—because yes, this is what I asked for. What I need.

"You're just a body now." He growls. "That's what you wanted, isn't it?" His hand fists in my hair, yanking my head back. "Say it."

Every thrust drives me into the wall. The elevator rocks slightly with the force of it, the slap of skin echoing off the metal.

"You like being taken like this?" His voice is a low snarl. "Anonymous. Mindless. Used."

I moan, body shuddering.

"You like being fucked in the dark?"

Each thrust slams into me, the sound of skin on skin echoing in the tight, dark space. I can't see his face. I can't see anything. And somehow, that makes it worse.

Or maybe... better.

Because in the dark, I don't have to lie. I don't have to pretend I'm not falling apart inside.

"Say it. Tell me this is what you want. To be used. To be fucked."

"Yes." I gasp as tension coils deep within me. "Take me."

"Fucking right I will."

His thrusts get harder. Faster. The elevator shakes with the force of it, his hips slamming into mine over and over as he strips me down to nothing but sensation and obedience.

And still, he doesn't stop.

This isn't about pleasure—it's about power, and for the first time in my life, I feel it the way I need to from a man.

Real. Raw. Right.

When I come, it's violent. My orgasm slams into me like a freight train, stolen from my body with precision I can't defend against. A sob rips from my throat, my whole body seizing, held up only by the wall and the man I said didn't matter.

I cry out his name—his fucking name.

"You said it didn't mean anything." He snarls. "Yet, you're sobbing my name."

And that's when he lets go, spilling into me with a groan that's anything but impersonal. Lucas comes with a raw, broken sound; one hand braced against the wall, the other still clamped tight to my hip.

He doesn't pull out right away. Just stays there, forehead pressed to the back of my neck, breath ragged.

The silence is deafening.

Just our breathing. Rough. Ragged. Syncing too fast.

I don't know what to say.

Because nothing about that was impersonal.

And we both fucking know it.

CHAPTER 6

THE COST OF CONTROL

LUCAS STEPS BACK SLOWLY, THE SEPARATION sudden and sharp. I feel empty in more ways than one.

He tugs his jeans up, runs a hand through his hair, and doesn't look at me.

"I shouldn't have done that." His voice is rough, full of something he rarely shows—regret. "That's not who I am." He mutters, shaking his head. "I lost it. I—fuck."

He rakes a hand through his hair, pacing the narrow space like he can outrun the guilt. "That was too far. I crossed a line. I knew you were spiraling, and I used it. I used you."

I try to catch my breath, but he's not done.

"It was wrong. And I'm sorry." He stops and turns to face the wall, jaw clenched. "It won't happen again."

Still no eye contact.

Still not looking at me.

"I promise you—whatever that was—I won't let it happen again." He's unraveling, words tumbling out fast and jagged. "I push, but I don't push like that. I don't take like that without checking in or asking. I turned sex into a weapon, and that's not fucking okay." His voice cracks, barely above a whisper. "I'm sorry."

I cross to him. One hand rises, hesitates, then lands on his shoulder.

He tenses beneath it. Like he doesn't think he deserves the touch.

"You weren't wrong," I say quietly.

His head turns slightly. Just enough that I know he heard me.

"You're right about all of it."

His shoulders rise and fall.

"I prefer sex when it's impersonal. I like it rough. Detached. Because when it's just a body and an orgasm, I don't have to feel anything. I don't have to open myself up to be hurt."

Again.

He turns fully now, his gaze cautious, lips parted.

"I've been keeping people at a distance—men at a distance, for a long time. Because someone once made me believe that needing more made me weak." I swallow. "So meaningless sex? That's safe."

Lucas opens his mouth, but I stop him with a hand to his chest.

"Last night wasn't meaningless." I whisper. "You're right. I lied when I said it was. I knew it before I even said the words."

Emotion flickers in his expression—wary, waiting.

"And what just happened?" I shake my head, unable to hold back the small, shaky laugh that escapes. "Lucas... I loved what you just did."

His brows pull together, confusion and disbelief clouding his features.

"I loved that you took." My voice drops. "That you weren't afraid to assert yourself. That you called me out on my bullshit. That you pushed me." I step closer, until there's barely an inch between us. "Punished me."

"If you don't believe me, then how do you explain my orgasm?" My gaze meets his, steady and exposed. "Because I came harder than I have in a long time. And it wasn't in spite of how you fucked me—it was because of it."

His jaw flexes, throat working around silence.

"I'm messy." I say. "And broken in ways I haven't figured out how to fix. But you can't take the blame for seeing me too clearly. Don't feel bad for giving me what I needed."

His brow furrows like he doesn't understand what I'm saying—like he can't understand how I could want what he just gave me.

So I step closer. Press a hand to his chest, right over his heart. Let him feel the truth.

"I've never met a man like you."

That gets his attention. His eyes flicker, guarded. But listening.

"I don't know why I'm wired the way I am. I've never trusted anyone enough to want more than the surface. It's easier with strangers. Guys who don't look too close. Because if they don't know me, they can't judge me."

A beat. A breath. Then I whisper the thing I've never said aloud.

"Because what gets me off? What I need? It's not soft or sweet or slow. It's being taken. Used. Made to feel like I don't have a choice. Like I'm a body to fuck and ruin."

He flinches.

But I don't stop. I can't. I need him to understand.

"With strangers, it's just sex. Just skin. They don't look at me the way you do." My voice catches. "You saw me, and you didn't pull back. You didn't flinch."

His eyes close, pain etched deep into every line of his face.

I press even closer, voice trembling. "I came apart because

of you. Because of how you held me. How you took from me. Not in spite of it—but because of it. You didn't just fuck me —you gave me something I've never had before."

His jaw clenches. But I see it now—the shift. The understanding. The recognition.

"I've never let anyone take control the way I did with you." I whisper. "Because I can only let go like that with strangers."

His brow tightens.

"Because when it's someone I don't know, I don't have to explain it. I don't have to feel bad for wanting what I want. There's no guilt. No weight. Just the act." I pause, breath shuddering. "But you... you didn't flinch."

His gaze sharpens, still quiet. Still holding back.

"You didn't recoil. You didn't pretend it was something it wasn't. You didn't coddle me or ask if I was sure halfway through."

I step closer until my chest brushes his. "You took what you wanted because you needed to take. Just as much as I needed to be used."

His breath hitches.

"And that?" I shake my head, my voice dropping. "That makes you the first man I've ever met with the balls to give me what I need. Not the illusion of it. Not roleplay. Not half-measures and safe words and let's-talk-about-it-after." My throat tightens. "You gave me the truth of it. The dark, dirty, dangerous realness of it. And you didn't look away."

His jaw flexes hard.

"I should be ashamed of what I want." I whisper. "But right now? The only thing I feel is relief. That someone finally saw all of it... and didn't run."

His hands fist at his sides like he's barely keeping himself together. But it's not guilt anymore.

It's heat.

And hunger.

Lucas doesn't move.

Doesn't blink.

For a second, I think he's going to push me away. Retreat. Shut down.

Instead, he steps in—slow and deliberate—until his chest presses to mine and his breath ghosts across my cheek.

"Don't romanticize what I did." His voice is low. Rough. Wrecked. "Don't rewrite it into something it wasn't just because it got you off."

I flinch. But I don't step back.

His hand curls around the back of my neck, not possessive—anchoring. "I do want to give you everything. The pain. The pleasure. The push and pull. I want to strip you down and rebuild you from the inside out. That's who I am."

He leans in, mouth at my ear. "But what I did?" A pause. A breath. "That was wrong."

I stiffen, but he keeps going.

"I didn't know your limits. I didn't ask. I didn't check in once." His voice shakes. "You gave consent in the past, sure. But in that moment? I took it. Assumed it. I crossed the fucking line because I was angry. I was angry last night didn't mean the same to you as it did to me. I wanted to hurt you, to punish you."

He pulls back just enough to look me in the eye, and what I see there isn't shame.

It's devastation.

"It doesn't matter that you came. Or that you wanted it." His jaw clenches. "It matters that we're still strangers. I haven't earned that kind of trust. I didn't protect you from myself when it mattered."

I swallow hard, throat thick.

"I need to own you, yes." He says, softer now. "But not like that. Not without rules. Without structure. Without making goddamn sure that you're safe while I take you apart and ruin you."

My breath catches.

His hand lifts, brushing my cheek, gentle like a man who knows he walked through fire and doesn't want to scorch me again.

"But..." I don't get it. He gave me everything I needed.

"I'll never cross that line again." His voice is reverent now. "Because I want to give you everything. But not at the expense of who I am."

He pauses.

"You want a man strong enough to take it all from you?" His eyes burn into mine. "Then you need a man who earns that right first. Not someone who crossed a line."

"But you didn't—"

"It may not be your line, but it most certainly is mine. I won't compromise who I am because I've found a woman who is everything I've ever needed in a woman."

"Lucas..."

He pulls me into his chest, wraps his arms around me, and holds on.

Not like a man trying to claim.

But like one trying to steady us both.

He holds me.

Not possessively. Not to make a statement.

Just... steady.

Silent.

I don't know how long we stay like that—wrapped in warmth and shared breath, surrounded by the faint hum of the elevator still stuck in limbo—but it feels like forever.

Then the lights flicker.

Once.

Twice.

A low hum builds under our feet as the machinery groans to life.

The elevator lurches with a metallic clank, and the sudden brightness overhead floods the space—too sharp, too much.

Lucas steps back like I've burned him.

I flinch, too, instinctively tugging the hem of the sweater down over my thighs. My legs are still bare, the borrowed pants forgotten somewhere on the floor between us.

His mouth opens slightly. Then closes again. Whatever was just between us—gone in a breath.

He bends, retrieves my pants without looking at me, and holds them out.

I take them from his hand without speaking.

He turns to face the panel and presses a button. The elevator shudders back into motion and rises.

I dress in silence.

So does he.

The air between us isn't tense exactly. It's just... unfinished.

The intimacy is still there, clinging to the corners like fog, but now it feels too visible in the light. Too real, but the silence is deafening.

The elevator doors glide open with a soft ding, spilling us into the top-floor hallway. It has plush carpet and dim emergency lighting humming overhead.

Neither of us moves.

I clutch the folded waistband of the leggings in my hands, suddenly very aware that I'm still reeling.

Lucas clears his throat.

When he finally speaks, his voice is flat. Calm. Professional. "I don't do messy."

I look up. His expression is unreadable. Closed off. Like last night, like the elevator, never happened.

"I want to be clear about what happened back there. That wasn't me. That isn't who I want to be. I don't use sex to hurt someone."

I swallow, chest tightening. "Lucas—"

"I let it get out of control. That's on me. And I don't like losing control. Not in business, and not with someone I'm supposed to be working with." He cuts me off gently.

His words land like ice cracking underfoot.

Clean. Final.

But it's what he doesn't say that guts me.

Not someone I care about.

Not someone I want.

Just... someone he's supposed to be working with.

A colleague. A complication.

Not the woman he held down and fucked like she was the only thing tethering him to this planet. Not the woman who let him inside in every way that matters.

And why should he? We were strangers before the storm. Two bodies and a blizzard. A few shared confessions and one brutal night that burned through every boundary I thought I had.

It's not supposed to be more.

But it feels like more.

And that's the real problem.

Because I'm standing here—skin marked, lips bruised, heart thudding out a rhythm that sounds suspiciously like stay —and he's already stepping back. Rewriting the rules. Reinforcing the line I shattered when I let him see the darkness I never share.

I should be grateful. Relieved.

But all I feel is cold.

"I think." He says, slower now, like it costs him something to say it. "We need to be clear with each other. No more sex. No more blurring the lines."

I nod, throat burning.

"Just work." He finishes. "You do your job, I'll do mine, and we make sure this wedding goes off without a hitch."

A beat.

"And when it's done." He says, voice soft, almost an afterthought. "We walk away clean."

Clean.

That word shouldn't feel like a knife. But it does.

"Okay." I manage, forcing the syllable out before my voice cracks. "You're right. It's better this way."

Lucas doesn't move for a moment.

Then his eyes meet mine—clear, steady, burning with something I can't name.

"It's not better, Amelia." He says quietly. "It's necessary."

The floor drops out from under me.

Because I hear it in his voice. The tension. The regret. The restraint.

He's not saying we're done because there's nothing between us.

He's saying it because there's too much between us.

Because what happened in that elevator wasn't just rough sex. It was a loss of control. A line blurred too far. And for a man like Lucas—who thrives on control and doesn't do messy —it rattled something deep inside him.

He's pulling away not because he doesn't want me. He's pulling away because he does. Because he wants it too much. And he's afraid of what could happen.

He turns and walks down the hallway, rattling off storm protocols, slipping back into business mode like armor.

But his shoulders are tense. His jaw clenched. His voice is a little too flat.

And I stand there, the echo of necessary ringing in my ears. Swallowing back everything I want to say and everything I shouldn't feel.

It's not a rejection. He is in a full-on retreat.

Not from me. From himself.

He's given me exactly what I asked for.

The top floor reveals no serious issues—just a few minor leaks easily tamed with towels and buckets. We fall into a rhythm, working side by side in silence. Not the strained kind, but something quieter. Heavier. As if the weight of what passed between us now hangs suspended between carefully drawn lines neither of us is willing to cross.

We speak only when necessary. Handing tools. Pointing out moisture. Agreeing on next steps.

Professional.

Efficient.

But every so often, I catch him looking at me—just for a second—like he's still trying to put the pieces back together in his head. The man in the dark. The man in the light. And where I fit between the two.

It's when we're taping plastic over the last leaky window that I ask—gentle, not probing.

"So why this place?"

He glances at me. "What do you mean?"

"You said you came here to renovate. Flip it." I gesture around us—exposed beams, hand-restored fixtures, the clear effort etched into every polished surface. "This doesn't look like a flip."

He straightens and wipes condensation from the inside of the window with the back of his hand. For a moment, I think he won't answer.

Then—quietly, "I never expected this place to become my life."

He gestures toward the floor-to-ceiling windows that frame the view beyond—mountains draped in snow, the hush of white-blanketed valleys stretching for miles.

"I came here to maximize my inheritance." He says. "Renovate. Sell. Pocket the profit. That was the plan."

I wait, not pushing.

"What changed?" I ask, softer now.

His eyes stay on the window, the view. Not me.

"I fell in love with it." He says. "With the quiet. With the solitude. With the purpose of building something instead of tearing it apart to make it more efficient."

His voice is steady, but there's a rawness to it. A truth that makes me feel like I've stepped into something private. Sacred.

"And now?" I ask.

His mouth lifts, just barely. "Now I'm too deep to walk away. I've sunk every dollar and hour I have into this place. I know every pipe, every board, every quirk. It's mine."

His gaze flicks to me. "It's not perfect. It's messy. Demanding. Stubborn as hell."

Then, just under his breath—so soft I almost miss it:

"Maybe that's why I stayed."

The words slip out like a secret not meant for me. But they land anyway. Hard.

I hear more than what he says—I hear what he means.

This place is messy. Demanding. Imperfect.

And worth it.

The sincerity in his voice resonates with something deep inside me. A place I've spent years barricading behind ambition and control. A place that's tired of being cold.

Because maybe I'm like this inn—renovated on the outside, crumbling beneath the surface. And maybe all this time, I've been searching for someone who wouldn't just gut me for parts. Someone who might stay because I'm difficult and messy.

Because I'm not easy.

Lucas turns toward me, unreadable.

"Come with me." He doesn't wait for an answer, just threads his fingers through mine like it's natural.

Easy.

And maybe that's the most shocking part—how right it feels.

He leads me down a narrow corridor I hadn't noticed before. The air is cooler here, and it's older. Every footstep feels hushed, reverent. The hallway ends at a simple wooden door with no label and no signage.

Lucas pulls out a small brass key. Unlocks it carefully.

"My grandfather built this for my grandmother." He says, voice low. "She loved stargazing."

The door swings open with a soft click.

Inside is a massive circular room. Every wall is paneled in warm cedar. A domed glass ceiling arches overhead, ringed with beams that seem to frame the sky itself.

Even in daylight, it's breathtaking.

I step inside slowly, mouth parted.

Though the sun still filters through pale clouds, I can already imagine the night—the sky ink-black, stars scattered like diamonds above us. A private observatory carved into the heart of a mountain.

"It's beautiful." I whisper. But the words don't come close.

He smiles but doesn't say anything. Just watches me with that quiet intensity again.

He brought me here not to impress me... but to see me. To show me something true.

"I come here when I need perspective." Lucas's fingers remain entwined with mine. "When the business challenges seem overwhelming, or I question whether I made the right choice staying."

"Do you? Question it?" I ask, suddenly needing to know.

"Sometimes." His honesty surprises me. "The resort operates on thin margins. We need this wedding to be successful—the publicity could transform our booking situation."

The admission creates an unexpected connection between us—both carrying the weight of professional pressure, both needing this event to succeed for different yet complementary reasons.

"We'll make it work." The words emerge with conviction I didn't know I possessed. "Whatever happens with the weather, we'll find a way."

Lucas's smile transforms his face, erasing the lines of worry. His hand tightens around mine, a silent acknowledgment of our unlikely alliance.

Through the glass ceiling, the clouds begin to part, revealing patches of brilliant blue. The storm has broken, at least temporarily. But as I stand beside this complicated man in the sanctuary he's shared with me, I realize another kind of storm is just beginning—one that might prove far more dangerous to my carefully ordered life than any blizzard.

And that storm is Lucas Reid.

CHAPTER 7

MELTING POINT

"No, NOT LIKE THAT." I REACH ACROSS THE TABLE, plucking the mangled napkin from Lucas's hands. "You're crushing the corners."

His sigh fills the resort's grand dining room, echoing off the vaulted ceiling. Outside, snow continues to fall in lazy spirals, adding to the three feet already blanketing Angel's Peak. Inside, we wage our own battle—me against Lucas's apparent inability to fold a simple napkin into a swan.

"It's a piece of fabric." He leans back in his chair, sleeves rolled to his elbows, revealing forearms corded with muscle. "Does it really matter what shape it's in? It's just going to end up in someone's lap."

I smooth the cream-colored linen across the polished mahogany table. "Details matter. The Mortons are paying for perfection, not 'good enough.'"

"Right." He reaches for another napkin from the stack I've meticulously arranged. "Show me again."

Morning in the atrium gave way to afternoon in the storage rooms. After discovering the resort's inventory system was as relaxed as its owner—meaning non-existent—I launched into an impromptu audit. Surprisingly, Lucas didn't object. Instead, he offered to help. Now, with supplies counted and emergency plans drafted, we've moved on to table settings.

I demonstrate the fold again, my fingers moving smoothly through the steps. "Bring the corner to the center, crease firmly, then fold back the sides to create the wings."

Lucas mimics my movements, his larger hands surprisingly nimble until the final fold, when the entire creation collapses into an unidentifiable heap.

"That doesn't look like a swan." He frowns at the crumpled fabric. "More like a swan that's been hit by a snowplow."

Despite my frustration, laughter bubbles up, escaping before I can suppress it. "That's possibly the worst napkin fold I've ever seen."

"You should've seen my attempt at origami in third grade." He grins, the expression transforming his face from merely handsome to devastating. "My paper crane looked more like a wounded pterodactyl."

"I believe it." I reach for his mangled creation, attempting to salvage it. "Here, watch closely."

Our heads bend together over the table, his shoulder warm against mine. The scent of his soap—something woodsy and subtle—fills my senses, momentarily distracting me from the task. My fingers falter on the fold as memories from last night and our elevator encounter surge unbidden. The heat of his body against mine, the commanding whisper of his voice in the darkness...

"Like this?" His question pulls me back to the present.

I blink, focusing on his latest attempt. It's still terrible—lopsided with uneven creases—but recognizable as bird-adjacent. Progress.

"Better." I can't help the smile tugging at my lips. "Though I wouldn't call it wedding-ready."

"How many of these do we need again?" He eyes the mountain of unfolded napkins like it personally offended him.

"Two hundred." I suppress a laugh at his horrified expression. "But we can probably manage with fifty perfect ones for the head tables and simpler folds for the rest."

"Thank God." He reaches for another napkin, determination etched in his jaw. "I was beginning to think we'd be here until next winter."

His next attempt ends in disaster—a mangled mess that looks more like a squashed bat than any kind of fancy fold.

"How is that even possible?" I stare at the lumpy shape in his hands, biting back a laugh. "You've defied the laws of physics."

"It's a talent." His grin is sharp and unrepentant. "One of my many useless skills."

"Along with running a resort with no guests?" I raise a brow, teasing.

"The Mortons were very clear. They wanted the entire lodge to themselves the week leading up to the wedding. Bought out every room." He doesn't miss a beat.

I blink. "A whole week? That seems... excessive."

"When you've got that much money to burn, privacy's just another luxury." He shrugs, folding another napkin like a man defusing a bomb.

"Guess mine's origami napkins and frostbite." I flash him a grin.

He glances up—just a flick of heat behind the deadpan. "And letting a complete stranger tie you to his bed."

My breath stutters.

His mouth twitches, not quite a smile. "But hey... some skills aren't useless."

I fold a napkin—badly—just to give my hands something to do. "I thought we weren't talking about that."

"We're not." He leans back in his chair, arms crossing as his eyes skim over me. "Just appreciating your commitment to hands-on hospitality."

Heat flares up my neck. I don't look at him.

And neither of us says what we're really thinking.

But the tension in the air?

That says plenty.

Flustered, I gather the napkins. "Maybe we should reconsider the elaborate place settings. Simple elegance might work better with the mountain backdrop anyway."

"I'm shocked." Lucas's eyebrows rise. "The perfectionist is compromising?"

The observation strikes closer to truth than I'd like to admit. "It's not compromise. It's... strategic adaptation."

"Is that what the kids are calling it these days?" He stands, gathering failed swan attempts. "Well, I fully support your strategic adaptation, especially if it means I never have to fold another napkin."

I smooth my hands over the stack of linens, unexpectedly lighter despite the work still ahead. "Maybe not everything needs to be perfect to be beautiful."

The words slip out unplanned, surprising me with their sincerity. Lucas pauses, his expression softening as our eyes meet across the table.

"Now that." He says quietly. "Is wisdom worth learning."

The moment stretches between us, charged with something beyond physical attraction, beyond our professional roles. Something that makes my heart beat faster in a way that has nothing to do with desire and everything to do with recognition.

The lights flicker, breaking the spell. Once, twice, then darkness falls as the generator fails completely.

"Well, that's inconvenient." Lucas's voice comes from the shadows. "Stay put. I know where the emergency lanterns are."

I remain at the table, listening to his footsteps retreat. Darkness presses against me, absolute and disorienting. Unlike our elevator encounter, there's no thrill in this blindness—only the practical concerns of managing a wedding with unstable power.

Lucas returns minutes later, the warm glow of an oil lantern preceding him. He sets it on the table, its light creating a small circle of warmth in the vast darkness of the dining room.

"The main generator's completely frozen." He places a second lantern beside the first. "I've got some space heaters running on battery power in my cabin, but we're looking at a cold night."

"What about the wedding? If we can't get reliable power—"

"We still have three days." He sits across from me, features golden in the lantern light. "The roads might clear tomorrow, and we'll get a repair crew up here. If not, I've got contacts with a helicopter service. We'll make it work."

His confidence should irritate me, but I find it oddly reassuring. "You're remarkably calm for someone whose entire business is at risk."

"Panic doesn't solve problems." He shrugs. "Besides, I've faced worse."

"Corporate takeovers?" I recall his mention of his previous career.

"Among other things." He leans back, shadows dancing across his face.

"You don't sound proud of it."

"I'm not." His admission carries the weight of hard-earned perspective. "I was good at it—ruthlessly efficient. Received bonuses based on how much I could cut while maintaining minimum service standards."

I try to reconcile this image with the man before me—the

one who splashed through puddles checking for leaks, who laughed over mangled napkins. "What changed?"

"Everything." His fingers trace patterns on the polished wood. "Eighty-hour work weeks. Living in hotels. Three relationships that couldn't survive my schedule and priorities."

The generator kicks back on briefly, lights illuminating the room before fading again, leaving us in the gentler glow of lanterns.

"We should move to the cabin." Lucas stands, gathering the lanterns. "It's warmer, and I've got some decent wine we can salvage from this day."

We bundle up against the biting cold, and the short walk to his cabin is a journey through a crystalline wonderland. Snow crunches beneath our boots, the night sky clearing to reveal a canopy of stars impossible to see in the city. My breath forms white clouds that dissipate into the darkness, each inhalation sharp with cold that burns all the way to my lungs.

Lucas's cabin welcomes us with residual warmth from the battery-powered heaters. He busies himself building a fire in the stone hearth while I shed my outer layers.

"You mentioned relationships that didn't survive your schedule." I settle onto the worn leather couch, watching him arrange kindling. "I've had similar experiences."

"Let me guess. They complained you were too driven, too focused on your career." The firelight catches the curve of his smile.

"Something like that." I tuck my legs beneath me, memories surfacing of arguments with exes who couldn't understand my dedication. "My last boyfriend said I loved my color-coded planner more than him."

"Was he right?"

The question lacks judgment, offered instead with genuine curiosity. "Maybe. I've built my reputation on perfection. It doesn't leave much room for compromise."

The fire catches, flames licking upward. Lucas straightens, dusting his hands on his jeans before disappearing into the kitchen. He returns with two glasses and a bottle of red wine.

"To imperfection." He hands me a glass of ruby liquid that gleams in the firelight.

I accept it, the glass cool against my fingers. "Is that a toast or an accusation?"

"Neither." He settles beside me, close enough that I feel the warmth radiating from his body. "Just an observation that sometimes the best things in life aren't planned."

The wine tastes rich and complex, warming me from within. "Is that your philosophy for everything? Just let things happen?"

"Not everything." His gaze holds mine, intensity simmering beneath the casual surface. "But I've learned control is often an illusion. The more desperately you cling to it, the more elusive it becomes."

Coming from anyone else, the statement would sound like new-age nonsense. From Lucas—a man who's mastered iron control in his corporate life and the art of letting go in his current one—it resonates with hard-earned wisdom.

"I'm not sure I know how to let go." The admission slips out quieter than I mean it to. Raw. Vulnerable. "Planning, organizing, anticipating problems—it's not just what I do. It's who I am."

"No. It's what you do." He shakes his head gently. "Not who you are."

His voice is calm. Certain.

That distinction lands hard.

Who am I without my color-coded schedules? My perfectly scripted contingencies? Without being the one who never cracks, never lets anything slip?

I don't realize I'm staring at the fire until I feel his eyes on me again.

Then—softly, a snort of laughter under his breath.

"I don't know." Lucas says, lips twitching. "Last night... letting go didn't seem to be a problem for you."

My head jerks toward him.

He's looking away—out at the mountains, not at me—but the smirk curves at the corner of his mouth, unmistakable.

And then it's gone.

That smile.

Wiped clean.

His voice drops.

"Not that it matters now."

It's not cold. Not distant. Just... final.

The kind of final that leaves no room for questions.

But I ask one anyway.

CHAPTER 8

THE LINE BETWEEN US

"Do you regret it?" I ask quietly.

His head turns slowly. Brows slightly drawn. "Regret what?"

"Drawing that line?" I lift a shoulder. Try to sound casual. Fail miserably. "Shutting it down before we had a chance to figure out what it was."

He doesn't answer right away. He just studies me like he's trying to decide if honesty is worth the risk.

Finally, he breathes out through his nose. Low. Frustrated.

"I don't regret the boundary." He says. "But I hate that I needed to make it."

That lands deep.

He looks away again, jaw tightening. "What happened in the elevator..." He pauses. Swallows hard. "That wasn't just about sex. It wasn't about control. I let myself go too far. You pushed—and I pushed back... harder. That's not who I want to be."

"I wasn't scared of you." I say softly. "You had my consent."

"That's not the point." The words crack like a whip, and

immediately, he curses under his breath. Closes his eyes. Breathes.

When he looks at me again, the control is back—but barely. It's frayed at the edges, barely holding.

Then the truth spills out—low and stripped of all defenses.

"I wanted to make it hurt. Not because you asked for it. Not because it turned you on. But because I was angry. I was humiliated. And for one second..." He swallows. "I wanted to punish you for it."

The air between us shudders.

His voice goes hoarse. "That's the line, Amelia. That's the part I can't live with. Not that you said yes. But that I didn't care. I wanted to hurt you. I knew you'd let me, and I used that to excuse it."

He looks down, hands flexing at his sides like he doesn't know what to do with them. "And like I said, you don't get to romanticize it or tell me it's okay. Because it wasn't."

Silence.

Heavy. Devastating.

He shakes his head once, then turns away.

I take a breath, the words scraping their way out. "Why?"

He stops, shoulders stiff.

"Why what?" He asks, without turning.

"Why were you humiliated?"

He goes still.

"Because you said it meant nothing." Then—quietly.

He turns then. Not angry. Just wrecked.

"I let myself believe it was more." His jaw flexes. "That it mattered, and then you looked me in the eye and threw it away like it was a transaction."

His words are a slap I can't flinch from. Because he's right. I did say that. I meant to say it.

But now?

I swallow the lump rising in my throat.

"I didn't know how to hold it." I whisper. "What it meant. What you made me feel. I've never had sex like that before. I've tried."

He doesn't speak.

I press on, the truth clawing free.

"No one's ever taken it from me like that." My voice is low, rough around the edges. "Not because I didn't give it—but because they couldn't."

I meet his eyes. Steady. Unflinching.

"I've tried. Men who said they were dominant. Who tied the knots, gave the commands, played the part. But it always felt like I was still in control. Like I was directing the scene from underneath it." I swallow. "It never worked. Not really. It was always just... pretend."

My voice drops. Honest in a way that guts me.

"But you—"

I step closer. My chest brushes his. I feel the heat of him. The gravity.

"You didn't ask. You didn't perform. You didn't pretend." My breath catches. "You just took. Like you already owned it. Like my submission was yours to claim. And the second you stepped into that space—everything in me recognized it. Like my body had just been waiting for someone strong enough to force the truth out of me."

My pulse pounds, and my breath trembles.

"You didn't just dominate me. You mastered me. And for the first time, it wasn't scary. It wasn't shameful. I didn't feel broken for needing it."

He doesn't move. Doesn't speak.

So I give him the last of it. The part no one else has ever heard.

"For the first time... I didn't feel twisted. Or warped. Or wrong. I didn't feel like a freak who needed to be fixed."

A pause. A breath.

"You made it feel natural. Like breathing. Like giving myself to you was the most instinctive thing I've ever done."

My voice thins to a whisper.

"You made me feel whole, and that terrified me. I wanted it too much."

He exhales, barely.

I step forward. "If punishment is what you need to layer on top of that—if hurting me made it easier to swallow what happened—I wouldn't have stopped you. I won't."

"Don't say that." His voice cuts like steel.

I blink, stunned by the sharpness.

"Why not?" I whisper. "Why can't I say it?"

He doesn't answer right away. His jaw clenches. Shoulders tense. Like he's holding something back with both hands.

"You know why."

"No." I say, stepping toward him. "I don't."

His gaze lifts to mine—and it's fierce. Not angry. Not cold. But feral.

"Because power without control—isn't control at all."

His voice echoes in the quiet, and the words hit like a warning and a wound all at once.

I don't breathe. I just stare at him, waiting—dreading— what comes next.

"I punished you in that elevator." He says, voice flat. His eyes meet mine, and there's no shame in them—only honesty. Brutal, raw honesty. "I meant for it to hurt."

My stomach twists.

"I wanted you to feel it." He goes on, steady now. "Not just the sex. The shame. The consequences. I wanted you to regret what you said. And I used your body to deliver that message."

I can't look away.

"But the mistake wasn't the act." He says. "It was that I didn't have the right to punish you."

His throat works like the words are clawing on their way out.

"You hadn't given me that yet. That trust. That surrender. The kind where punishment means something more than pain." He steps closer, eyes locked on mine. "I claimed something I hadn't earned. I crossed a line, not because you didn't consent—but because I hadn't been given authority to correct. And I took it anyway. It doesn't matter that you gave it after the fact."

My chest tightens—my pulse hammers in my throat.

"And that." He finishes softly. "Is what I can't return from."

The breath whooshes from my lungs.

He looks at me then. No armor. No masks.

Just him.

"That's not control." He says. "That's cruelty wearing the same skin."

I open my mouth, but the words catch. Stumble.

Because now I see it—the guilt. The war inside him that he's been barely keeping in check. Not rage. Not regret over wanting me.

But over what he became in the wanting.

And still, I can't let it end here.

Not without asking.

"Is there any way..." I pause, swallow, and find the courage. "Any way we could come back from it?"

The question hangs there between us. Heavy. Naked.

His face doesn't change, not much—but his shoulders rise, just slightly, as if the effort of holding himself together suddenly doubled.

And then, he shakes his head once. Just once.

"It's too little." He says, voice tight. "Too late."

The words land like a door slamming shut.

Not in anger. Not even sadness.

Just finality.

I nod slowly, the weight of his words sinking through my skin and into my bones.

The words are final.

And they hollow me out in one clean sweep.

I nod slowly, throat burning. "So that's it then? We pretend it didn't happen?"

He doesn't answer right away.

He stares past me like he's afraid that if he looks again, he'll come undone, too.

"No. We don't pretend." He meets my gaze. His voice softens. "We remember exactly what it was. And we leave it where it belongs."

The ache in my chest pulses.

I force a nod. "Okay."

For a long moment, we sit there—quiet, breathing the same air, watching the fire crackle and cast golden shadows along the stone hearth.

Then Lucas leans forward and downs the last sip of his wine. He refills his glass first, then gestures toward mine. I nod. He pours.

When he settles beside me again, his shoulder brushes mine—close, but not quite touching.

He stares into the fire for a beat before speaking.

"Where'd it start?" His voice is soft. Curious, not confrontational. "This need to be perfect all the time?"

I blink, caught off guard by the question. By the fact that he's not pushing, not dissecting—but genuinely wants to understand.

"I don't know." I admit, curling my fingers around the warmth of my glass. "Maybe... always? It was just easier. To get praise. To avoid conflict. To be useful."

He nods like he understands more than he lets on.

"So you became the one who holds it all together."

"Exactly." I murmur. "And if I'm not perfect, I lose value. If I fall apart—"

"You're human." He says simply. Then he reaches for my hand, collecting it in his.

I look at him. The way firelight softens his profile and carves shadows across his jaw.

"And that's allowed?" I ask, only half-joking.

He doesn't smile.

"It has to be."

"That's terrifying." I manage a shaky laugh.

"Most worthwhile things are." His thumb traces circles on my palm, sending shivers up my arm that have nothing to do with cold.

The fire crackles, throwing shadows across the cabin's walls. Outside, the world remains frozen, but in this small space, something is thawing—not just between us but within me.

"My turn for a confession." Lucas refills our glasses. "This resort is struggling financially. I've poured everything into renovations, believing success would follow if I built something special."

"Has it?"

"Not yet." His honesty surprises me. "We have good summer bookings, but winters are lean. This wedding could change that—exposure in all the right publications, word of mouth among the social circles that matter."

Understanding blooms. "That's why you're so calm about the setbacks. You need this to succeed as much as I do."

He nods, firelight playing across the angles of his face. "Different motivations, same goal."

"Partners by necessity." I raise my glass in a small toast.

"Could be worse company to be stranded with." His smile holds warmth that seeps into places long cold.

We talk as the fire burns lower, sharing stories of professional triumphs and disasters. I tell him about the celebrity wedding where the bride's train caught fire (quickly extinguished, crisis averted). He counters with the corporate retreat where the CEO's secret affair with the CFO became painfully public. The wine bottle empties as laughter fills the cabin.

When I finally set my glass aside and attempt to stand, my legs have stiffened from hours on the couch. Lucas rises first, extending his hand.

"Careful." He steadies me as I wobble. "The floor's uneven here."

His warning comes too late. My foot catches on the edge of the rug, sending me pitching forward. His arms wrap around my waist, preventing a fall but drawing me flush against his chest. My hands brace against his shoulders, feeling the solid strength beneath the soft flannel of his shirt.

Time suspends. His heartbeat pulses against my palms, strong and slightly accelerated. My own races to match it. Unlike our previous encounters—raw and primal, driven by physical need—this moment carries a different weight, a tenderness that terrifies me more than desire ever could.

His eyes search mine, asking a question I'm not sure I want to answer. One hand rises to cup my cheek, thumb tracing the curve of my lower lip gently.

"Amelia." My name emerges as a whisper, a question, a prayer.

When it comes, the kiss bears no resemblance to the hungry claiming of before. This is achingly tender, a soft press of lips that asks rather than demands. I answer without thought, leaning into him, my hands sliding up to cradle his face.

The contact deepens gradually, a slow melting rather than a conflagration. His arms tighten around me, not with possession but with reverence. My fingers thread through his hair, learning its texture, memorizing the spot at the nape of his neck that makes him sigh against my mouth.

We break apart slowly, foreheads pressed together, sharing breath in the quiet space between one moment and the next. The fire has burned to embers, casting the room in a soft, golden light that seems to exist outside of time.

"That was..." I struggle to find words for something I've never experienced before.

"I know." His voice holds wonder that matches my own.

Something fundamentally shifts between us—a boundary crossed that has nothing to do with physical intimacy and everything to do with vulnerability. In his arms, feeling the gentle press of his lips against my temple, I'm in danger of losing more than my professional distance.

I'm in danger of losing my heart.

The room stays suspended in that golden hush, the air thick with breath, memory, and something too fragile to name.

His lips brush my temple one last time before he exhales— a sound full of restraint like he's trying to tuck something unruly back inside himself.

Then his arms loosen.

He steps back.

The loss of his warmth is immediate. Devastating.

"I'll take the couch." He says softly, not quite meeting my eyes.

The words slice deep, carving through the echo of the kiss still lingering on my mouth.

Right.

The line.

Still there.

Still standing.

Even after that.

I shake my head. "No, I'll take the couch."

"You don't have to do that." His head snaps up.

I give a small, tired smile. "Consider it my punishment."

"We're not doing that." His jaw tics.

"You're right. We're not doing that. I am. Consider it self-imposed punishment." I meet his gaze. "It feels fair to me. You're too big for that couch anyway."

He opens his mouth to protest, but I cut him off, softer now.

"I see your line, Lucas." My voice doesn't shake, even though my heart does. "And I respect it."

A pause. A breath.

"But I'm not going to give up."

His eyes darken. With what—I don't know. Anger? Longing? Fear?

Maybe all three.

But he doesn't speak.

And that silence tells me everything.

I grab a throw from the armchair and curl up on the couch, facing the back cushions. The fire crackles behind me, and his footsteps retreat—measured and heavy.

I listen to the creak of the bed.

I hear him move.

Then stop.

Then nothing.

But sleep doesn't come easy for me.

Not when I can still feel his kiss ghosting over my lips.

And not when I know—absolutely know—

This isn't over.

CHAPTER 9

DAMAGE CONTROL

MORNING LIGHT FILTERS THROUGH THE CABIN windows, painting golden stripes across the rumpled sheets. I blink awake, momentarily disoriented by the unfamiliar surroundings, before memories of last night flood back. The tender kiss by the firelight. The way Lucas held me afterward, neither of us pushing for more. The quiet goodnight as he retreated to the bed, and I slept on the couch.

My fingers drift to my lips, still sensitive from his kiss. So different from our previous encounters, less about physical dominance and more about... connection. The shift unsettles me more than I care to admit.

"Focus, Amelia," I mutter, throwing back the covers. Today is about wedding preparation, not the complicated thing between me and the resort owner.

The cabin is quiet as I dress. There is no sign of Lucas in the kitchen or living area. Just a note propped against the coffee pot: *Gone to check generator. Coffee's fresh. Help yourself.*

Relief and disappointment war in my chest. Professionalism wins—this distance is exactly what we need. Whatever happened last night was an anomaly, a momentary lapse fueled by isolation and wine. Today, we return to being professionals with a job to accomplish.

I pour coffee into a ceramic mug emblazoned with the resort logo, the rich aroma momentarily drowning my complicated thoughts. Outside, the world remains transformed by snow, pristine white stretching to the horizon. Beautiful, but isolating.

The cabin door opens with a rush of frigid air, revealing Lucas stamping snow from his boots. His cheeks are flushed from the cold, and his dark hair is dusted with crystalline flakes that catch the light. Our eyes meet across the room, and for a moment, everything else falls away.

"Morning." He breaks the silence first, shrugging out of his heavy coat. "Sleep well?"

Such an ordinary question carries so much subtext. "Yes, thanks. Any luck with the generator?"

"Some good news and bad news." He pours himself coffee, maintaining a careful distance between us. "I've got the generator functioning again, but the weather report isn't promising. Roads will be closed for at least two more days."

My stomach drops. "Two days? That puts us right against the wedding deadline."

"The plows are working around the clock, but the accumulation is significant." He sips his coffee, eyes studying me over the rim. "We should check the main building for any new damage from overnight freezing."

"Right." I set down my mug. "I'm concerned about the reception hall with those high ceilings and older windows."

We bundle up against the cold, and the walk to the main resort building is conducted in professional silence. The tension from last night has evolved into something more complex—not awkwardness exactly, but a heightened awareness. Every accidental brush of the shoulders feels deliberate. Every exchanged glance carries weight.

The resort's grand entrance hall welcomes us with restored electricity, lights gleaming against polished wood and stone. At least something's going right. However, as we approach the main reception hall, the sound of dripping water grows increasingly ominous.

I push open the double doors and freeze in horror. Water cascades down one wall where a massive window meets the ceiling, pooling on the hardwood floor below. Ice has forced a gap in the sealing, allowing melting snow to penetrate. Already, dark stains spread across the carefully restored flooring.

"No, no, no." I rush forward. "This is catastrophic. The reception is supposed to be here."

Lucas examines the damage without the panic that currently has my heart hammering against my ribs. "It's not as bad as it looks. The water damage is localized to this corner."

"Not as bad?" I gesture wildly at the spreading pool. "This room is the centerpiece of the wedding reception. It's featured in every plan, every layout, every discussion with the clients."

Rather than matching my escalating tone, Lucas remains calm. "We'll handle it. First, let's stop the active leak."

He disappears, returning minutes later with maintenance tools and materials. I watch in conflicted admiration as he efficiently seals the gap, stopping the immediate water intrusion. His competence both impresses and irritates me—shouldn't he be more concerned about this disaster?

"The floor will need professional restoration." He says, kneeling to examine the damaged wood. "That won't happen before the wedding."

"So we're doomed." I sink onto a chair, mind racing through inadequate contingency plans.

"Or." Lucas stands, brushing dust from his knees, "We use the Mountainview Room instead. It's slightly smaller but has better natural light and a more intimate feel."

"The Mountainview Room wasn't in any of the plans." I resist the immediate rejection my perfectionist tendencies demand, forcing myself to consider alternatives. "Show me."

He leads me through corridors to a room I hadn't noticed during our initial tour. Double doors open to reveal a space with floor-to-ceiling windows along one wall, offering breath-taking views of snow-covered peaks. The room has a warmth the grand reception hall lacks, with rich wood paneling and a massive stone fireplace at one end.

"It's beautiful." I admit, mental calculations already rear-ranging tables and decorations to fit the new space.

"And more practical for winter weddings." Lucas moves to the fireplace, checking that it's operational. "The heating is more efficient here, and the views are unmatched."

I pace the perimeter, measuring steps and visualizing the transformation. "I need to rearrange the seating chart completely. The dance floor would work better near the windows. The head table would face this way instead..."

Lucas watches me with something like admiration. "You're already seeing it, aren't you? The whole event reconfigured in your mind."

"It's my job." I continue my assessment. My professional focus momentarily displaces personal fears. "It could work. We'd need to document the changes thoroughly for the client's approval."

"I'm sure they'll understand, given the circumstances." He joins me at the windows, close enough that I can feel the heat radiating from his body.

"You don't know Charlene Morton." I turn to face him, suddenly aware of our proximity. "She's had this wedding planned since childhood. Every detail matters."

Something shifts in his expression—a softening around the eyes, a subtle curve of lips. "Sounds like someone else I know."

The observation lacks mockery, offered with gentle understanding that disarms my defensiveness. "We're not alike. She's driven by fantasy, and I'm driven by excellence."

"And never the twain shall meet?" His voice holds amusement.

"Occasionally, they overlap." I step back, needing distance to maintain professional focus. "Let's inventory what we'll need to transform this space. I'll draft alternative layouts while you handle the technical elements."

We fall into surprisingly effective teamwork, moving around each other without conscious coordination. I draft new seating arrangements while Lucas assesses the room's lighting capabilities. I recalculate table placements while he tests the sound system. The tension between us remains, but transforms into something productive—energy channeled into creative problem-solving rather than awkward avoidance.

Hours pass in focused work, and the room gradually takes shape. By late afternoon, we've created a comprehensive plan that improves upon the original design. The smaller space feels more intimate and romantic, better suited to a winter wedding than the cavernous reception hall.

"We should document the changes," I suggest, surveying our work with cautious satisfaction. "I need to send updates to Miranda and the client."

"Use my phone." Lucas offers his device. "Better camera than yours."

I accept it, snapping photos of the room from various angles. The results are underwhelming—flat images that fail to capture the room's potential.

"These aren't going to convince anyone." I scroll through the inadequate photos, frustration mounting. "They can't see what we're envisioning."

"Let me try." Lucas takes the phone, adjusting settings

before approaching the first shot differently. "Photography was a serious hobby of mine before the resort took over my life."

He moves through the space purposefully, finding angles I never considered, capturing how light plays across surfaces. I watch, fascinated by this new dimension of skill, another layer to the increasingly complex man before me.

"Check these." He hands the phone back, our fingers brushing briefly.

The difference is striking. Where my photos showed an empty room, his captures potential—the majestic mountain backdrop, the warm intimacy of the space, and the way the late-afternoon light creates golden pools on the polished floor.

"These are..." I search for a word that won't inflate his already considerable ego.

"Professional quality?" He suggests with a grin.

"Adequate." I counter, fighting a smile. "But we need more. Every element that's changing needs documentation."

"Then let's do a proper session." He takes the phone back. "We'll stage key elements, get samples of the linens and center-pieces, really show how it will all come together."

The prospect of continued collaboration both thrills and unnerves me. "How about food first? I'm starving."

We retreat to the resort's kitchen, raiding supplies for an impromptu meal. Lucas proves as competent at cooking as photography, whipping up pasta from ingredients salvaged from the walk-in refrigerator. We eat at the prep counter, discussing wedding logistics interspersed with companionable silence.

My phone rings just as we finish—Miranda's name flashes on the screen. I answer, dreading the conversation.

"Please tell me you've made progress." Her voice crackles through the less-than-perfect connection. "The Mortons are hounding me for updates."

"We've had some challenges with the venue." Despite

Lucas watching me intently from across the counter, I keep my tone professionally neutral. "Water damage in the main reception hall."

"Water damage?" The connection can't disguise her horror. "Amelia, this wedding cannot fail. The Mortons are threatening to pull all future business if their daughter's day isn't perfect."

"We've developed an alternative plan using another space in the resort. It's more suitable for a winter wedding." I gesture for Lucas to send the photos to my email so I can forward them.

"The Mortons don't want alternatives. They want what was promised." Her voice rises, stress evident.

"I understand, but—"

"No buts. Fix this, Amelia." The call disconnects before I can respond.

I set the phone down carefully, aware of Lucas's observant gaze. "That went well."

"Your boss sounds charming." His dry tone pulls a reluctant laugh from me.

"Miranda's under pressure, too. This wedding represents millions in future business." I check my email, relieved to see Lucas's photos in my inbox. "These are impressive. Really impressive."

"Let's get more." He stands, gathering our dishes. "A full portfolio to showcase the new plan."

The next hours transform into an unexpected adventure as we move through the resort, staging and photographing elements of the revised wedding plan.

Lucas proves to be a patient teacher, showing me how to find the best angles and use available light. What begins as a necessary documentation exercise evolves into something playful as we rearrange furniture, experiment with table settings, and occasionally disagree on artistic direction.

"No, the flowers need to be lower." I adjust a sample centerpiece for the tenth time. "Guests need to see each other across the table."

"But the composition works better with height." He frames the shot, his brow furrowed in concentration.

"Function over form." I nudge his shoulder, the casual contact sending unexpected warmth through me.

"Says the woman who wanted fifty identical napkin swans." His retort comes with a smirk that shouldn't be as attractive as it is.

Our banter continues as we work, the professional purpose increasingly interwoven with personal connection. I laugh more than I have in months. The rigid perfectionism that usually governs my work softens in the face of his creative approach.

"One more location." Lucas checks his watch as we finish in the Mountainview Room. "I want to show you how the atrium looks at sunset."

We return to the glass-domed space he showed me yesterday, now transformed by the setting sun. Golden light pours through the glass ceiling, painting the circular room in warm amber tones. The snow-covered mountains beyond glow pink and purple in the fading light, creating a breathtaking backdrop that momentarily steals my voice.

"Imagine a ceremony here." Lucas speaks quietly, as if reluctant to break the magic of the moment. "Just before sunset, with the mountains turning gold and purple. Candles lining the perimeter, flowers along that curved wall."

The vision forms in my mind with startling clarity—not just any wedding, but a fairytale brought to life.

Intimate, magical, unexpected.

"Oh my god, that would be perfect." The words escape in a whisper. "Better than perfect. It's a fairytale wedding come to life. She's going to freak out when I show her these pictures."

"Better than perfect?" He turns to me, eyebrows raised in mock surprise. "Who are you, and what have you done with Amelia Hayes?"

Excitement builds as I move through the space, my mind racing with possibilities. "We could hold the ceremony here at sunset, then move to the Mountainview Room for the reception. It creates a natural flow, and this space—Lucas this space is magical."

"You're magical right now." His quiet observation stops me mid-stride. "Watching you see possibilities instead of problems. Creating beauty from unexpected challenges."

Something shifts in my chest—a recognition, a surrender to the joy of creation over the tyranny of perfection. Without thinking, I cross to him, hands gripping his shoulders as I bounce with excitement.

"We can do this. We can make it even better than the original plan."

Energy pulses through me, bright and unfiltered—professional momentum braided tightly with something far more personal. More dangerous.

Lucas's hands settle at my waist, grounding me. His touch isn't firm. Isn't possessive. It's steady. But the heat behind it? That burns.

Our eyes lock.

The air shifts.

The excitement between us morphs into something heavier. Deeper. The kind of pull that has nothing to do with logistics or client satisfaction and everything to do with us.

His gaze drops to my lips. Intent clear. Breath catching.

My heart lurches.

Maybe this is it.

Maybe this moment, in the center of something beautiful we discovered together, is enough to draw him across that line.

To remind him that not everything born in the dark has to stay there.

I lean in slowly, giving him the chance to stop it.

He doesn't.

His breath ghosts across my skin, warm and wanting.

My eyes flutter closed.

And then—

Darkness.

Complete and absolute.

The atrium's lights vanish, swallowed by the sudden power failure. Only the faint glow of twilight filters through the glass dome above, outlining our silhouettes in silver-blue.

I inhale sharply, blinking against the black.

Lucas steps back.

Just one step.

But it feels like a chasm.

"I should check the generator." He clears his throat.

The spell is broken.

The kiss never happened.

And the line between us?

Still there.

Still holding.

Even when I'm standing right on the edge...

Reaching for him.

"Timing." Lucas murmurs, his voice a mixture of frustration and amusement. "Always about timing."

The interrupted moment hangs between us, unresolved yet undeniably present. Like the wedding plans we've been revising, something has fundamentally changed—not ruined, but transformed into something unexpected.

Perhaps, like the new wedding design, something even better might come out of the mess I made of things between us.

CHAPTER 10

UNEXPECTED ALLIES

CHAPTER 10: UNEXPECTED ALLIES

I spend another night on the couch.

A lumpy, too-short, spine-killing couch that smells like cedar and restraint.

Lucas and I are still at odds when it comes to anything personal.

Professionally?

Professionally, we're kicking ass and taking names.

The glass dome of the atrium glows with morning light; the sunlight fractures into a kaleidoscope of rainbows that scatter across the floor like confetti. I sit cross-legged in the middle of it, phone pressed to my ear, pretending I slept more than three hours and didn't wake up aching—in more ways than one.

The power's back. For now. So is cell service. I've spent the past hour going over every detail of the revised wedding layout with Miranda. Lucas's photos—stunning, moody, impossibly romantic—finally broke her down.

"Well." She sighs after a long pause. "I hate to admit it, but the new venue might actually be an upgrade."

I don't bother hiding my smile. "Told you."

But the moment the words are out of my mouth, the satisfaction fades.

Because while our client gets her dream wedding, I get to camp on a couch six feet away from the man I can't stop thinking about. His body off-limits. His boundaries etched deeper with every near-miss.

I press my hands into the small of my back, stretch, and try not to groan.

He didn't even offer to switch last night.

Not that I would've said yes. But still.

The floor creaks behind me—Lucas's footsteps, precise as ever—and I school my face into something that doesn't scream sexually frustrated lunatic.

It's fine. It's all fine.

After all, I'm only planning someone else's happily ever after...

While sleeping on a couch.

Alone.

In Lucas's shirt.

"I'm impressed with your adaptability, Amelia." Miranda's words snap me back to the present. Her words carry faint praise wrapped in surprise. "The Mortons have tentatively approved the changes, pending final details."

I lower the phone and roll my shoulders, trying to work out the kink in my neck from another night spent twisted on Lucas's couch like some kind of determined house cat.

The worst part? I didn't even argue about it.

After the power outage cut short our almost-kiss in the atrium—because apparently the universe loves to cockblock me—we retreated to the cabin in silence. Not strained. Not angry.

Just... awkward.

Neither of us acknowledged what nearly happened. For the second damn time.

And now? The pattern is becoming painfully familiar.

Moments of closeness. Real connection. Heat that hums like a live wire between us.

Then distance. Retreat. A muttered goodnight and separate sleeping arrangements like we're coworkers on a church retreat.

Correction: I'm not the one afraid of it. I'm team Full-Steam-Ahead. Open arms, open heart, open bed.

Lucas?

He's team Full-Stop.

Captain Line-in-the-Sand. And heaven forbid either of us step a toe over it.

It's infuriating.

Not just because I want him—which I do—but because he wants me back. I see it in every look that lingers too long, in how his voice dips when he says my name, and how his hands settle at my waist like it's instinct.

And then he yanks himself back like he's been burned.

Like I'm the fire.

Spoiler alert, Lucas—I'm just the tinder. You're the fire, and I need you to make me burn.

I'm starting to lose patience with playing the role of something dangerous he needs to resist.

"Amelia? Are you listening to a word I'm saying?"

"I'm sorry, Miranda what did you say?"

"The Mortons have tentatively approved the changes."

Relief washes through me. "That's wonderful news. We—"

"Hold, please." Her voice cuts off, replaced by muffled conversation.

Sure, because I have nothing to do but hold for her. It's not like I'm preparing for the marriage of the century.

"Amelia?" Miranda's voice returns, tight with fresh tension. "I have Charlene Morton on the other line. There's a situation."

My stomach drops. "What kind of situation?"

"She wants to change the menu. Specifically, she's insisting on adding her grandmother's signature chocolate soufflé for dessert. Apparently, it's a family tradition she suddenly can't live without."

I close my eyes, counting to five before responding. "The menu was finalized months ago. The resort has already ordered all ingredients."

"I'm aware." Miranda's tone suggests she's already had this conversation. "But the bride is distraught. Crying on the phone. Her grandmother passed recently, and this is now a non-negotiable element."

Of course, it is because nothing about this wedding could possibly be simple.

"Let me speak with her."

A click, then Charlene's voice fills my ear, punctuated by theatrical sniffles. "Amelia? Please tell me you can make this happen. It's the only last-minute thing I've asked for, and it would mean everything to have Grandma Rose's soufflé at my wedding."

I bite back the observation that she's asked for at least seventeen "last-minute" changes since we began planning. "Charlene, I understand this is important to you. Do you have the recipe?"

"Of course. I'll email it right away. It's very specific— the chocolate has to be a particular French brand, and there's a special vanilla bean infusion that makes it uniquely hers."

Specialty ingredients. During a blizzard. With all the roads closed.

Perfect.

"I'll see what I can do." I keep my voice professionally neutral. "No promises, but we'll explore every option."

By the time I end the call, Lucas is standing in the doorway, leaning against the frame, casual and just-showered in a way that should not be legal this early in the morning.

His damp hair curls slightly at the ends, a dark, tousled mess that begs to be tugged. A towel hangs carelessly around his neck, catching droplets that trickle down the strong column of his throat, disappearing beneath the cling of a long-sleeved black thermal that fits entirely too well.

And those sweatpants?

Grey. Loose. Low on his hips.

Unforgivable.

My eyes betray me—trailing down, pausing at the sharp cut of his obliques where shirt meets waistband, then skimming the long lines of his legs until I force them back up. His arms are crossed now, muscles flexing beneath the fabric that hugs every inch like it was stitched for sin.

He raises an eyebrow, amusement flickering across his face as if he knows exactly where my brain has gone.

"Problem?" He asks.

Yes.

You.

In that shirt.

Looking like a walking contradiction of restraint and ruin.

But I clear my throat and offer a smile that's definitely more grimace than grace.

"The bride wants to add her late grandmother's chocolate soufflé to the menu." I rise to my feet, brushing imaginary dust from my borrowed jeans. "With specialty ingredients, we don't have, can't order, and can't access because we're snowbound on a fucking mountain."

Instead of the expected commiseration, Lucas's eyes spark with interest. "What kind of ingredients?"

I glance down as Charlene's email pings. "Valrhona chocolate, Tahitian vanilla beans, some special French butter I can't pronounce, and..." I scroll, "orange flower water? Is that even a real thing?"

"It is." He steps closer to peer over my shoulder, the clean scent of his soap curling around me like a trap. "This doesn't look impossible."

I turn to face him, instantly distracted by how close he is —his height, his heat, the quiet intensity in his gaze.

"We're stranded in a blizzard." I snap, trying to keep my footing. "Everything is fucking impossible right now."

"Language." His eyes flick down to mine, calm but sharp.

The single word lands like a gloved hand at the back of my neck—soft, but commanding. Not angry. Not judgmental. Just a quiet assertion of boundaries.

Of control.

A flicker of heat curls low in my belly.

Of course, he'd find a way to reassert control with one damn word.

I swallow. "Sorry."

"It's fine. Just don't take it out on the mountain." His mouth quirks. Just slightly.

His smile holds a hint of the arrogance I found so irritating days ago, now somehow transformed into something almost charming. "I know a guy with a helicopter service in Ridgeline. We've worked together before on supply emergencies."

"You're suggesting we helicopter in soufflé ingredients?" I can't keep the incredulity from my voice. "That seems... excessive."

"Says the woman who wanted hand-folded swan napkins for two hundred guests." His teasing lacks the edge it might have had days ago. "Besides, we need fresh supplies anyway. The roads won't open for at least another day, maybe two."

Hope stirs despite my attempts to remain realistic. "Would your contact fly in this weather?"

"Jason flew combat missions in Afghanistan. A little mountain snow is nothing." Lucas pulls out his phone. "Let me make the call. In the meantime, let's see what ingredients we do have. We should test the recipe before the wedding day anyway."

An hour later, Lucas has not only arranged for a supply drop but somehow convinced his friend to prioritize the specialty ingredients Charlene's recipe requires. I'm torn between admiration for his problem-solving and irritation at how effortlessly he seems to handle crises that would send me into a spiral of anxiety-fueled planning.

"Delivery scheduled for three this afternoon, weather permitting." He pockets his phone as we make our way to the resort's industrial kitchen. "Jason's already got most of the ingredients at his base. He does supply runs for several high-end resorts in the area."

"I'm impressed." The admission costs me nothing, I realize with surprise. "That was quick thinking."

"I've had practice with mountain emergencies." He pushes through the kitchen's double doors, flipping on lights that illuminate gleaming stainless steel workstations. "You learn to adapt, or you don't survive up here."

The kitchen stands ready and immaculate, designed to serve hundreds of guests at capacity. Now, with just the two of us in the cavernous space, it feels like we've stumbled into someone else's life—playing chef in a restaurant after hours.

Lucas strides ahead, already rolling up his sleeves. He doesn't hesitate.

"Apron." He grabs one from a hook and tosses it to me without looking. Then hands himself another and ties it around his waist efficiently. "We'll take inventory first. I want to see what we're working with before we start guessing."

I catch the apron mid-air, a little stunned at the sudden shift in command.

But I follow his lead, tying the strings around my waist as he moves like he's done this a thousand times. Calm. Controlled. Entirely at home.

"My chef preps for worst-case scenarios. We should have most of the basics." He opens one industrial fridge, scanning shelves.

I fall into step behind him, trying not to trip over the change in tone.

He's no longer the emotionally distant man avoiding couches and kisses—he's the boss now. Precise. Focused. Utterly in his element.

And I am not okay.

Because this?

This right here—Lucas in full command, quietly issuing instructions like it's second nature—is the exact version of him I've been begging for. Not out loud, obviously. But somewhere deep in my lizard brain, the part that short-circuits every time he says language in that voice, or steps a little too close and looks a little too hard...

This bossy kitchen commander thing?

Yeah. It's my own personal porn.

He moves like authority itself, and it makes my breath hitch—not from exertion, but from want.

I want his control. His attention. That sharp, quiet confidence that says he knows exactly what he's doing.

It's maddening.

He walks around like this is nothing—like he hasn't been drawing hard emotional boundaries and pretending what happened between us was some unfortunate blip.

Now he's tossing aprons and directing inventory like he's not holding the blueprint to every one of my goddamn fantasies.

I clear my throat. "You always this bossy in the kitchen?"

He glances at me. Smirks.

"You always this easily flustered by competence?"

I set the measuring cup down harder than necessary, flour puffing into the air like smoke off a fuse.

"I'm flustered by your damn line in the sand." I snap, throwing a hand in the general direction of the kitchen—and maybe the universe. "You walking around here, all calm and competent and in charge, tossing aprons like you don't know exactly what that does to me?"

His brow arches, but I'm already on a roll.

"You bossing me around is my fantasy, Lucas."

His head tilts, eyes narrowing just slightly.

"I thought it was tying you to my bed."

Heat surges up my neck, but I don't flinch. I don't back down. Not anymore.

"To your bed." I fire back. "To those damn rings overhead. To the ones on the posts. It's not the rope, Lucas. It's you."

His breath hitches, but I keep going, my voice rising with every word.

"It's you taking control. Forcing me to take it. Forcing me to stay still and feel it. You know what that does to me—how fast I fall apart when you stop letting me pretend I'm not dying for it."

He steps closer, jaw tight. That storm behind his eyes cracks wide open.

"I'm not trying to make things complicated." I say again, but this time my voice breaks. "But you've been walking around like you're the only one going through hell, and I'm just... collateral."

My fists clench at my sides. "It's driving me insane."

His hands slam down on the counter between us, and he leans in.

"You're not the only one going insane."

The words are low. Controlled. But beneath them is a shout.

"The last two nights?" He growls. "Hell. I've been lying in bed hard for you. Fucking hard. Knowing you're six goddamn feet away on that couch, and I can't touch you. Can't fuck you. Can't claim you the way I want to."

My mouth falls open.

"So don't stand there and act like I haven't been wrecked every goddamn second you breathe near me." His eyes blaze.

The silence is electric. Shaking.

And then, I exhale.

"Then do it." My voice shakes with the force of it, the rawness. "Take me. Right here. Right now. Just stop this torment."

Lucas doesn't move.

He doesn't breathe.

His jaw clenches, muscles in his throat working like he's swallowing down a war. And for one agonizing second, I think he might crack. That he'll cross the space between us and destroy me in the best possible way.

But instead, he steps back.

The distance is a knife.

"I won't. And you damn well know why." His voice is low, controlled—unyielding.

"No." My breath shudders out. I shake my head, tears burning hot in the corners of my eyes. "No, you don't get to do that. You don't get to say you want me. That you're hard for me. That I'm driving you insane—and then refuse to touch me."

His jaw clenches. His silence says enough.

"Tell me how that's fair." I demand, voice cracking. "Tell me why it's okay for you to want me like that—say it like it's breaking you—and still pull back every time we get close."

He watches me. Quiet. Impossibly still. And when he

finally speaks, his voice is low and precise. Like every word is weighed before it's allowed to exist.

"If you want me to be in charge..." He steps forward. Slow. Controlled. His breath brushes my cheek. "To really be in charge..." He leans close, lips at my ear, tone like a blade sliding between ribs. "Then this is our punishment."

A pause. A beat.

"Our punishment?" My breath catches.

Chapter 11

Hot Whisks and Cold Showers

"We moved too fast." Lucas murmurs. "We let the storm do the deciding. If you want a man who takes control then you need one who doesn't let his darkness swallow you with him."

He leans forward, his presence overwhelming even as he remains impossibly composed. His breath is warm against my ear as he whispers, "Until the wedding is done—until every detail is locked down—we focus on work. Consider this our punishment. A reminder that, despite everything, I have to hold the line. No distractions. No more."

His words sink deep. Heavy. Final.

And just like that, the storm shifts.

Not the one outside—but the one inside me. The one I've been feeding with heat, hope, and the desperate need to close the distance between us.

He doesn't leave me room to argue. Doesn't offer softness or apology. Just cold clarity and consequence.

I say nothing.

Not because I agree.

Because I understand.

This is what it means to want a man like Lucas:

You don't just get the fire.

You get the restraint. The rules. The sharp edge of discipline when you push too far.

He watches me a beat longer, making sure I've absorbed it all.

Then—calmly, like nothing just fractured between us—he speaks.

"Now." He says, his voice smooth as steel. "If you're done..."

A pause. Just enough for the words to land.

"I suggest we focus on the emergency of the hour..." He turns toward the prep station, rolling up his sleeves like this is any other day. "Let's whip up a soufflé."

I grab a whisk and mutter just loud enough for him to hear, "Well if that doesn't get a girl all hot and bothered..."

Lucas laughs. A deep, low sound that skates across my skin like warm breath on bare thighs.

"Careful." He says without looking up. "Say things like that, and I'll have to add another day to your sentence."

I choke on my own breath. "My sentence?"

"Punishment. Sentence. Call it what you want." He shrugs, all casual menace, as he unpacks a tin of imported cocoa.

"You're unbelievable."

"That's not what you were calling me two nights ago."

My cheeks flare with heat. "Don't test me."

"Too late." He lifts a brow, sliding the cocoa across the counter toward me.

We fall into an unexpectedly comfortable rhythm, moving around each other in the large space like nothing just detonated between us. Like we didn't just toe the edge of something we both want too much.

I read requirements from the recipe while Lucas locates

items, occasionally suggesting substitutions for things we're missing. His knowledge of food and preparation surprises me.

"So, how did you learn to cook?" I measure flour into a bowl, creating a small cloud of white dust.

"By necessity." He cracks eggs single-handedly, talk about skill. "Growing up, it was just my dad and me after my mom left. He worked long hours, so I either learned to cook or lived on cereal."

The casual mention of his mother leaving drops like a stone in still water, ripples of unspoken history spreading outward. I wait, sensing there's more to the story if I give him space to tell it.

"My grandfather bought this place back in the day." Lucas continues, focusing on separating egg whites from yolks. "Everyone thought he was crazy—former mining lodge with rotting floors and a leaking roof. But he saw its potential."

"Like grandfather, like grandson." The observation slips out unbidden.

His smile holds a touch of melancholy. "He died before he could finish the renovations. Heart attack while shoveling snow, ironically enough. I was in my first year at business school."

"I'm sorry." The words feel inadequate for the loss I hear beneath his matter-of-fact tone.

"The resort was his dream, not mine. I was chasing corporate success, seven-figure bonuses, and corner offices. I nearly sold this place a dozen times." Lucas shrugs, but the deliberate casualness doesn't quite mask the emotion.

"What stopped you?"

"Memories, at first." He measures vanilla into a small bowl, the rich scent filling the space between us. "Then, gradually, I started seeing what he saw—a place that could bring joy and create moments that matter. Something real in a world of corporate artifice."

I absorb this glimpse into what shaped him, understanding blooming like the deep notes of vanilla in the air. "Your grandfather's atrium. Your grandfather's vision. No wonder this place means so much to you."

"Most people just see a business decision—why not sell to a hotel chain and cash out?"

He glances up, surprise flickering in his expression.

"I'm not most people." The words emerge softer than intended.

"No." His gaze holds mine across the kitchen island. "You're definitely not."

Then he glances down, catches the mess I've made of the flour, and chuckles low in his throat.

"You really suck as a sous chef."

I arch a brow, wiping flour from my wrist. "Yeah? Well, there's one thing I suck pretty damn well—"

"Jesus, Amelia." Lucas groans, head tipping back like he's praying for strength.

"Just trying to be helpful." I grin wickedly, licking a dab of batter from my fingertip. "Just because I'm being punished... doesn't mean you need to suffer."

His eyes snap to mine—dark, focused, dangerous.

"You know damn well." His voice is low and lethal. "If I let you suck my cock, what'll happen next."

I freeze. My breath stutters.

"Don't try and manipulate me, and if it happens again..." He leans in, not touching me, but close enough that I feel the heat of his words on my skin. "I'll add even more time to your sentence."

I gape at him. "You can't be serious."

"Oh, I'm dead serious."

"You're punishing me for offering to make you feel good?" I fold my arms.

"Actions have consequences." He shrugs one shoulder.

I scowl at him like a brat denied candy. "This is cruel and unusual."

"Discipline is rarely convenient."

My whole body hums with want. Frustration. The sense that I've walked into a game I cannot win—and never want to stop playing.

Because underneath the sexual frustration is something else entirely. Something that lights me up from the inside like a live wire. The way he talks about punishment, discipline, consequences—it's not empty roleplay or bedroom games. It's real. He means it. And the fact that he's willing to enforce actual discipline, to hold firm boundaries even when I'm practically begging him to break them?

It's deliciously, dangerously wonderful.

I mutter under my breath, "Bet your cock's not suffering half as much as I am."

"Keep pushing, sweetheart. I dare you." Lucas smirks.

The tension between us stretches taut again—hot, charged, filthy—just shy of snapping.

And then—

The thrum of rotors cuts through the stillness, vibrating through the windows, the ceiling, and our skin.

"Jason's early. I'll go handle the delivery."

Lucas straightens, checking his watch, expression hardening into something cool and alert. All business again.

"Of course." I mutter, throwing my hands in the air. "This damn place. If it's not the generator going out, it's a goddamn helicopter."

"Excuse me?" His brow lifts as he moves toward the door.

"This place is a goddamn cockblock."

He stops in his tracks and laughs—low, full, and completely unrepentant.

"Welcome to your sentence, sweetheart." Lucas turns and walks out of the kitchen.

"It would've been worth it." I shout after him.

He laughs, and like that, he's gone—leaving me in a puddle of heat, flour, and sexual frustration.

He disappears, leaving me with half-mixed ingredients and thoughts too complex to untangle. When he returns minutes later, arms laden with supplies and cheeks flushed from the cold, I've managed to compose myself into a professional again.

"Let's see if these fancy ingredients are worth the trouble." I unwrap the chocolate, inhaling the rich aroma. "Though I must admit, this smells promising."

We work side by side, following Grandmother Rose's detailed instructions. The kitchen fills with heavenly scents as we whip, fold, and stir. When Lucas reaches past me for a utensil, his arm brushes mine, sending an unreasonable flutter through my stomach. I focus harder on the task, increasingly aware of his presence in a way that has nothing to do with our professional collaboration.

The first test batch emerges from the oven looking distinctly un-soufflé-like—a flat, sad disc that draws matching frowns from both of us.

"We overmixed." Lucas pokes the deflated dessert with a spoon. "Knocked all the air out."

"Let's try again." I reach for fresh ingredients, determined to master this challenge.

Three attempts later, we produce a passable soufflé, though still not quite matching the picture Charlene sent. Lucas studies it critically, head tilted.

"The texture's wrong. We need a lighter touch with the folding."

"Show me." I hand him the spatula, watching his large hands incorporate the ingredients delicately.

"Like this." He demonstrates the gentle folding motion. "More of a cut and turn, not stirring."

I mimic his movement, concentrating so intently that I don't notice the streak of flour on my hand until it's too late. As I tuck a strand of hair behind my ear, Lucas's lips twitch with suppressed amusement.

"What?" I glance up from the bowl.

"You've got a little..." He gestures vaguely toward my face, eyes dancing with mischief.

I reach up, feeling the telltale powder across my cheek. "Very mature. Are you going to tell me there's something on my shirt next?"

"No need." Without warning, he deliberately dabs a fresh smudge of flour on the tip of my nose. "Now you match."

For a heartbeat, I'm too stunned to react. Then outrage bubbles up, followed immediately by an unfamiliar playfulness. I retaliate by flicking egg white from my fingertips directly onto his shirt.

"Oh, it's like that, is it?" His expression of exaggerated shock only encourages me.

Before I retreat, he scoops a handful of powdered sugar and blows it gently in my direction. The white cloud settles across my hair and shoulders, turning me into a winter apparition.

"You did not just—" I grab the nearest weapon—a bottle of vanilla—and shake droplets at him, leaving dark speckles across his formerly clean shirt.

What follows can only be described as culinary warfare.

Flour flies.

Egg white splatters.

And chocolate smears across countertops.

Lucas's deep laughter echoes off the stainless steel surfaces as I dodge behind a workstation, seeking ammunition. I can't remember the last time I engaged in something so utterly childish and delightful.

"Truce." He finally holds up his hands, his face streaked with cocoa and hair dusted white. "I surrender."

I emerge from behind my makeshift barricade, breathless with laughter and equally covered in ingredients. "Look at this disaster. We're supposed to be professionals."

"Speak for yourself." He grins, reaching out to brush sugar from my cheek. "I'm just a humble innkeeper."

"And I'm a sexually frustrated wedding planner with an unfair sentence." I lean into his touch despite myself.

"Unfair?" His thumb traces along my cheekbone, eyes darkening. "You love the discipline as much as you need the incredible sex."

My breath catches. Because he's not wrong.

His touch lingers, warm fingers against my skin. The laughter fades, replaced by something quieter, more intense. For a moment, I think he might kiss me—I want him to kiss me—but he steps back, clearing his throat.

"We should clean up."

The kitchen restoration takes twice as long as the mess-making, filled with companionable conversation as we work. Lucas shares stories of his grandfather's early days running the lodge, of the property's evolution over the decades, and of his reluctant journey from corporate predator to preservationist.

I find myself sharing, too—my childhood fascination with organizing, my mother's elaborate dinner parties that sparked my career, and the satisfaction of creating perfect moments for clients.

"You never talk about yourself." Lucas wipes down a final counter as I load the dishwasher. "Always the job, never the woman behind it."

"The job is safer." The honesty surprises me. "Clearer boundaries and well-defined expectations."

"Who is Amelia Hayes outside of work?" His question holds genuine interest.

I consider deflecting, then find myself answering truthfully. "She's... a work in progress. Less certain than she appears."

"I like her." His simple statement warms something cold and dormant inside me. "Both versions."

My phone rings before I can respond, Miranda's name flashing on the screen. I answer with apprehension, knowing her calls rarely bring good news lately.

"Please tell me you've solved the soufflé situation." Her voice carries the strained patience of someone nearing their breaking point.

"We have the ingredients and are testing the recipe now." I move toward the window for better reception, lowering my voice. "We'll have it perfected before the wedding."

"Good. Because the Mortons..." Her tone sharpens. "We both know what that would mean for your future at Elite Events."

The implied threat lands as intended. "I understand."

"Do you? Because if this wedding fails, your career at Elite is over. No Paris promotion, no future with the firm at all. Everything you've worked for—gone." The connection crackles with static or perhaps just the chill in her voice. "Don't disappoint me, Amelia."

I end the call, hand trembling slightly as I set the phone down. When I turn, Lucas stands closer than expected; his expression hardened into something I haven't seen before—the corporate shark surfacing beneath the mountain innkeeper.

"Your boss is a real piece of work." His voice holds controlled anger. "Threatening your career over circumstances beyond anyone's control."

Heat rushes to my face. "You were eavesdropping?"

"Not intentionally, but I heard enough." He steps closer,

protective indignation radiating from him. "Does she always manipulate you like that?"

"It's not manipulation. It's business." I straighten my spine, defensive despite my misgivings about Miranda's tactics. "The Mortons are major clients."

"That doesn't justify threatening someone who's moved mountains—literally—to salvage their event." His eyes narrow, calculating in a way that reminds me of his former corporate life. "What's this about Paris?"

I hesitate, then sigh. "A promotion. Running Elite's new European division."

"Is that what you want?"

The question catches me off guard with its simplicity. Is it what I want? I've been so focused on achieving it and proving myself worthy that I've barely considered whether the goal aligns with my desires.

"It's a tremendous opportunity." I sidestep the actual question. "Career-defining."

"That's not what I asked." Lucas studies me with unsettling perception.

Before I can formulate a response, the kitchen lights flicker ominously. We both glance upward, holding our breath until the electricity stabilizes.

"Storm's picking up again." Lucas moves to the window, peering at the darkening skies. "We should head back to the cabin before we lose power completely."

The walk to the cabin is a battle against strengthening winds and snow swirling in chaotic patterns that steal breath and obscure vision. When we reach the door, we're both shivering despite our heavy coats.

Inside, Lucas immediately builds a fire while I prepare hot drinks. The flames gradually warm the small space as daylight fades outside, snow accumulating against windows that are already half-buried. We eat a simple dinner; our conversation carefully steered toward wedding preparations rather than the more personal territory we'd been approaching.

When the dishes are cleared and we're running out of practical topics, Lucas glances toward the bedroom. "You should take the bed tonight. I've noticed you rubbing your neck after sleeping on the couch."

"We could share." The suggestion emerges before I can analyze its wisdom. "The bed's enormous, and we're both adults."

"Are you sure?" His eyebrows lift slightly.

"Strictly practical." I maintain a matter-of-fact tone despite the sudden dryness in my throat. "We both need proper rest to handle whatever tomorrow brings."

He studies me for a moment, then nods. "Practical."

The bedtime routine unfolds carefully—separate bathroom use, changing in private, deliberate space maintained between us as we settle under the covers. The mattress dips with his weight, the sheet pulling slightly taut between us like a border neither dares cross.

I sleep under the sheets. He sleeps on top of them. An effective, if not infuriating barrier. Once settled in, Lucas covers us both with two layers of blankets. I've never been so close to a person I literally can't touch.

Darkness envelops the room as Lucas extinguishes the bedside lamp. Only the faint glow from the fireplace in the other room filters through the partially open door, casting elongated shadows across unfamiliar terrain. I lie rigidly on my side, hyperaware of his presence mere inches away—the subtle rhythm of his breathing, the faint warmth radiating across the no-man's-land of sheet between us.

This is absurd. We've shared far more intimate contact than sleeping in the same bed. Yet somehow, this feels more vulnerable and meaningful than the passionate encounters that came before. Those could be dismissed as physical responses or isolation-induced attraction. This quiet coexistence requires a different kind of trust.

"Amelia?" His voice emerges soft in the darkness.

"Yes?" I whisper back, irrationally afraid of disturbing the stillness around us.

"Thank you for making this work, despite all the chaos. The resort really needs this wedding to succeed."

His simple gratitude warms me more than any physical contact could. "Thank you for being so adaptable to the changes."

The silence stretches between us, comfortable rather than awkward. Outside, the wind howls against the cabin walls, reinforcing the cocoon-like intimacy of our shelter. The mattress shifts slightly as Lucas turns toward me.

"Goodnight, Amelia." The word carries more weight than its two syllables should allow.

"Goodnight, Lucas."

I close my eyes, listening to the storm outside and his quiet breathing beside me. For the first time since arriving at Angel's Peak, I feel neither anxious about the wedding nor confused about my attraction to Lucas. Instead, a curious peace settles over me—the recognition of having found an unexpected ally in what began as adversarial territory.

Sleep approaches gradually, my awareness of his proximity never fading. In the last moments before consciousness slips away, I realize with startling clarity that the most dangerous aspect of this arrangement isn't the risk of physical boundaries crossed between us, but the emotional ones. Because somewhere between professional antagonism and reluctant collaboration, Lucas Reid has become something I never anticipated.

Essential.

CHAPTER 12

REALITY CHECK

THE VIBRATION OF MY PHONE AGAINST THE
nightstand jolts me from sleep. In the gray pre-dawn light, I
fumble for it, careful not to disturb Lucas's sleeping form on
the other side of the bed. We've maintained our careful
distance throughout the night, though I woke once to find his
hand stretched toward me in sleep, fingers just inches from
mine.

"Hello?" I whisper, slipping from beneath the warm
covers.

"Ms. Hayes?" An unfamiliar male voice crackles through
the connection. "This is Sheriff Donovan. I'm calling all the
stranded guests and staff at Angel's Peak."

I move to the bedroom doorway, pulling it nearly closed
behind me. "Yes, what is it?"

"Good news. The plows have made significant progress
overnight. We expect the main access road to be cleared
enough for staff vehicles and essential deliveries by late afternoon today."

The information should bring relief. Instead, my stomach
twists with sudden anxiety. "Today? You're certain?"

"Barring any new complications." Pride colors his voice. "The boys have been working around the clock. Thought you'd want to know since I understand there's a big wedding happening soon."

"Yes, thank you." I end the call and stand motionless in the dim cabin, processing the implications.

The roads are opening. Staff will arrive today. The wedding machine will lurch into motion. The peaceful bubble we've existed in for days will burst, replaced by the chaotic reality of a compressed timeline and a mountain of logistics.

My pulse quickens, my mind racing through everything that must happen in a precise sequence. We've lost critical setup days. The new venue needs a complete transformation. The menu changes require chef consultation. The floral deliveries will arrive without proper staging time. The—

"Morning." Lucas's voice interrupts my spiraling thoughts.

He stands in the bedroom doorway, sleep-rumpled and unfairly attractive in a faded T-shirt and flannel pants. His hair sticks up at odd angles, and stubble darkens his jaw. The casual intimacy of seeing him this way—guard down, defenses absent—sends an unwelcome flutter through my chest.

"The roads are clearing." I gesture with my phone, my voice sounding strained even to my ears. "The sheriff says staff and deliveries can get through by late afternoon."

"That's good news." Lucas nods, moving toward the kitchen, infuriatingly calm.

"Good news?" I follow him, incredulous at his reaction. "Lucas, we have a day and a half to execute a complete wedding. We've lost nearly all our prep time. The venue has changed. The menu has changed. Nothing is going according to plan."

"Plans change. We adapt." He fills the coffee maker, movements practiced, seemingly unconcerned by my mounting panic.

"How can you be so calm about this?" I pace the small kitchen, energy coursing through me with nowhere to go. "This wedding could make or break your resort's reputation. Not to mention my entire career."

"Panicking won't help either of those things." He turns to face me, leaning against the counter as the coffee begins to brew. "We've done the hard part—solving the major problems. Now we just need to execute and follow through."

"Just?" I nearly choke on the word. "There's no 'just' about it. We have hundreds of details to coordinate in half the normal time."

The coffee maker gurgles to completion as Lucas regards me steadily—that gaze that both irritates and steadies me. "And we will. One step at a time."

He hands me a steaming mug, our fingers brushing in the exchange. The brief contact grounds me momentarily, pulling me back from the edge of complete panic.

"I need to shower and change." I cradle the mug, drawing strength from its warmth. "Then make about fifty calls before the staff arrives."

"I'll handle the lodge preparations." Lucas sips his coffee, watching me over the rim. "I'll make sure all systems are operational, and all the spaces are cleared and ready."

His calm competence should reassure me. Instead, it highlights how we approach problems differently—his steady adaptability versus my need for meticulous control. Yet somehow, over these past few days, those differences have become complementary rather than conflicting.

The thought settles me as I retreat to prepare for the day ahead. By the time we walk to the main lodge, I've armored myself in professionalism—hair pulled back, my day-before-the-wedding 'suit' as neat as possible, and all my mental checklists arranged in precise order of priority.

The first vehicles arrive shortly after noon, crunching over gravel and packed snow. Staff members I've only met through email introductions materialize in physical form—the executive chef and his team, florists laden with preserved arrangements, logistics coordinators with tablets and concerned expressions.

I meet them at the entrance with a clipboard in hand and a Bluetooth headset in place. "Welcome to Angel's Peak. We have significant adjustments to the original plan, so please hold all questions until I've completed the overview briefing."

What follows is a masterclass in crisis management, if I do say so myself. I direct teams to their stations, outline the venue changes, distribute updated timelines, and address concerns authoritatively. Years of handling last-minute wedding disasters have prepared me for exactly this moment—when control seems impossible but must be maintained anyway.

Lucas works the room differently, moving between teams effortlessly, smoothing ruffled feathers when my directives come too sharp, and providing context where my brevity leaves gaps. We orbit each other without direct coordination, somehow sensing where the other is needed, filling spaces the other leaves open.

"The pastry chef is stuck in Ridgeline with a broken-down van." A harried kitchen assistant appears at my elbow while I review floral placement with the design team. "Chef Morgan says we can't do the soufflé without him."

Before I can respond, Lucas materializes beside us. "I know a mechanic in Ridgeline. Give me the details."

While he handles that crisis, I pivot to address a delivery error with the linens—the wrong shade of ivory, requiring rapid steam treatment to brighten them to acceptable levels. The problem-solving dance continues through the afternoon —a missing sound system component here, a staffing gap there, each challenge met with solutions cobbled together from resources at hand.

"You're good at this." Lucas appears at my side during a rare quiet moment, voice low enough that only I can hear. "Better than good. Exceptional."

The unexpected praise warms me more than it should. "So are you. For someone so 'relaxed' about planning."

His smile holds a hint of pride—not in himself, I realize with startling clarity, but in me. "Different methods, synergistic results."

We're interrupted by the executive chef, who needs to make immediate decisions about the revised menu timing. I follow him to the kitchen, where chaos reigns as staff unpack deliveries and establish workstations. The confident chef resists my insistence on checking every element.

"With all due respect, Ms. Hayes, I've been preparing high-end events for twenty years." Chef Morgan crosses his arms, bristling at my suggested adjustments to his workflow. "My team knows what they're doing."

"And I'm responsible for ensuring every detail meets the client's expectations." I stand my ground, though he towers over me by nearly a foot. "The timeline has compressed significantly. We need redundancies built in."

"My kitchen, my methods." His expression darkens. "Mr. Reid has always trusted my judgment."

"Everything alright here?" As if summoned, Lucas appears behind me.

"Your event planner is micromanaging my kitchen." Chef Morgan's accent thickens with irritation. "It disrupts our established system."

I turn to Lucas, expecting him to side with his staff member. "I'm simply ensuring we have contingencies for every element, given the compressed timeline."

To my surprise, Lucas's expression hardens, his easy-going demeanor replaced by something sharper, more reminiscent of the corporate executive he once was. "Chef, a word?"

They step aside for a brief, intense conversation. I catch fragments—"exceptional circumstances" and "professional courtesy"—before the chef returns with a begrudging nod of acceptance.

"We will incorporate your... suggestions." He manages a tight smile. "Though I maintain they are unnecessary."

"Thank you." I match his professional tone, refusing to gloat. "I appreciate your flexibility."

As the kitchen team resumes work, Lucas gestures toward a quiet hallway away from the bustle. I follow, preparing arguments for my approach, certain he's about to lecture me on staff relations.

The moment we're alone, his controlled expression gives way to frustration. "You can't come into my resort and dictate to staff who have worked here for years."

"I can when the success of this event depends on precision and execution." I match his intensity, keeping my voice low but firm. "Your chef was dismissing my concerns because of his ego."

"And you were overriding his expertise because you need to control every detail." Lucas steps closer, the hallway suddenly feeling much narrower. "Sometimes you have to trust people to do their jobs."

"Trust?" The word emerges as a scoff. "I trusted the weather would cooperate. I trusted your staff would be here three days ago. I trusted the venue wouldn't spring leaks. Look where trust has gotten us."

"Exactly where we need to be." He gestures sharply toward the bustling main areas. "Working together, finding solutions, creating something better than the original plan."

"That's not because of trust. It's because of contingency planning and quick thinking." I step forward, refusing to be intimidated by his proximity. "If I just trusted everything would work out, we'd be facing disaster right now."

"If you trusted the people around you, you might not be constantly on the edge of burnout." His words hit precisely. "There's a difference between high standards and destroying yourself to meet impossible expectations."

His hand wraps around my upper arm, not painful but firm—a physical emphasis to his words that sends heat cascading through me. For a heartbeat, I think he might pull me closer and finally break the careful distance we've maintained. His eyes darken, dropping briefly to my lips before he visibly reins himself in, releasing my arm and stepping back.

The charged moment stretches between us, neither advancing nor retreating. Finally, understanding dawns clearly. This isn't about control versus flexibility. It's about trust in each other, in the strange partnership we've forged through the crisis.

"You're right." The admission costs me nothing, I realize with surprise. "I need to trust more, but you must understand why that's difficult for me."

Something softens in his expression. "I do understand. Perfection is your armor."

The simple observation strikes uncomfortably. Before I can respond, a staff member calls for Lucas from the main hall —another crisis requiring attention.

"We should get back." I smooth my shirt, rebuilding my professional composure.

"For what it's worth, I trust you. Completely." Lucas catches my hand before I can turn away.

The words settle like a weight and a gift simultaneously in my chest. "I trust you too."

We return to the chaos with a new understanding, making our coordination even more seamless. When the kitchen team hits a snag with the revised menu, I defer to Chef Morgan's expertise while offering suggestions rather than directives. When the floral team struggles with placement in the new venue, Lucas backs my vision without hesitation.

Hours blur together as late afternoon fades to evening. Staff come and go in shifts, progress visible in the gradually transforming spaces. The Mountainview Room evolves from empty potential to stunning elegance, while the atrium takes shape as a magical ceremony venue.

By midnight, only a skeleton crew remains, with most staff retiring to newly accessible accommodations in town. Lucas and I continue working side by side, reviewing progress and finalizing details for the next day's push. Our earlier tension has transformed into comfortable collaboration, punctuated by moments of shared humor over particularly challenging solutions.

"You need to eat something." Lucas appears at my elbow as I review seating charts for the twentieth time. A tray is in his hands—a midnight picnic amid wedding chaos.

"I'm not hungry." My stomach immediately betrays me with an audible growl.

"Your body disagrees." His laugh is low and warm in the quiet space.

We settle in a corner of the Mountainview Room, surrounded by half-dressed tables and stacked chairs. The wine is rich and earthy, and the food is simple but exactly what my body needs after hours of neglect.

Our shoulders touch as we lean over documents, the contact neither awkward nor intentionally intimate—just comfortable proximity between two people who have somehow crossed the boundary from adversaries to partners.

"Look around." Lucas gestures with his wine glass at the space taking shape around us. "Twenty-four hours ago, this was a contingency plan. Now it's going to be more beautiful than the original venue."

I follow his gaze, allowing myself to see not what still needs to be done but what we've already accomplished.

"We did this."

"You did." His smile in the dim light does something peculiar to my pulse. "Against impossible odds."

"Nothing's impossible with the right plan." I counter automatically, then amend: "And the right people to execute it. You're being generous with your praise. I could never have done this without you."

His hand finds mine on the table, fingers intertwining with casual intimacy that feels new and familiar. "Want to see something?"

He leads me through the quiet resort to the atrium, now softly illuminated by strings of fairy lights. The florists have begun their transformation, with greenery and early arrangements framing the circular space. Above, the glass dome reveals a clearing sky where stars glitter against the backdrop of retreating storm clouds.

"They've done amazing work." I move to the center of the room, turning slowly to take in the progress.

"It was your vision." Lucas remains by the doorway, watching me with an expression I can't quite decipher. "You saw what this space could become."

"We saw it together." I tilt my head back, gazing up at the canopy of stars beyond the glass. "This might work."

"It already is." His voice comes softer and closer as he moves to stand beside me.

Our eyes meet in the gentle light. The moment stretches, fragile and perfect—a bubble of possibility suspended between what was and what might be. Neither of us moves to break it; perhaps we're both afraid of what will happen when reality returns.

Dawn finds me in the lodge's small lounge, curled in an armchair after only an hour of restless sleep. My mind refuses to quiet, racing with tasks, contingencies, and unspoken questions about what will happen when the wedding ends and we return to our separate lives.

Lucas appears in the doorway, freshly showered and looking rested despite our late night. He pauses when he sees me, then enters with two steaming mugs.

"Thought you might need this." He offers coffee, and our fingers brush in the exchange.

"Thanks." I cradle the warmth between my palms, breathing in the rich aroma. "Big day ahead."

"One more day." Lucas settles into the chair across from me, his eyes holding mine over the rim of his mug.

I nod automatically, mind already cataloging seating charts and vendor check-ins. "I know. Final dress steaming, rehearsal timeline, dinner setup—everything has to run like clockwork."

He doesn't respond right away. Just watches me. Steady. Quiet.

I frown slightly, mistaking his silence for stress. "Hey— we've got this. It's all coming together."

But when I glance up again, something about his expression tugs at me. Like he's on the edge of saying something else —something not about table linens or flower deliveries.

Still, I push forward, already mentally reordering the to-do list. "And then it's showtime."

My voice is bright. Too bright.

He lifts his mug again. Takes a slow sip. Says nothing.

The silence stretches—gentle, but taut.

Outside, dawn spills over the peaks, painting the untouched snow gold and blush pink. The storm has passed, but somehow, the air feels heavier than before.

One more day.

I file it away as a reference to the wedding and completely miss how his eyes follow me when I look away.

CHAPTER 13

UNDER PRESSURE

A CONVOY OF LUXURY VEHICLES SNAKES UP THE freshly plowed mountain road, their polished surfaces gleaming in the midday sun. I stand at the resort entrance, shoulders squared and smile fixed, as the wedding party begins to arrive. After a day and a half of frantic preparation, the moment of truth has arrived—and with it, my boss.

Miranda steps from a sleek black SUV, her tailored wool coat and designer boots immaculate despite the journey. Her critical gaze sweeps over the resort exterior, cataloging imperfections only she can see. Her lips press into a thin line of disapproval when her steely gaze lands on me.

"Amelia." She air-kisses my cheek, the scent of her exclusive French perfume momentarily overwhelming. "You look... rustic."

"Blizzard chic." I attempt humor while gesturing toward the entrance. "Everything is prepared for the Mortons' arrival. They should be in the next vehicle."

"I certainly hope this last-minute venue change won't disappoint them. The original reception hall was a key selling point." Her eyes narrow slightly.

Before I can respond, Lucas appears at my side, the picture of confident hospitality in a tailored charcoal sweater and dark jeans. "You must be Miranda. I'm Lucas Reid, owner of The Haven."

"Mr. Reid." Her professional smile emerges, the one reserved for important clients and potential revenue sources. "I understand we have you to thank for accommodating our event despite the weather challenges."

"The credit belongs to Amelia." His hand rests briefly at the small of my back, a subtle show of support that doesn't escape Miranda's notice. "Her adaptability and vision transformed what could have been a disaster into something truly special."

"Is that so?" Miranda's eyebrows lift slightly.

"Absolutely. Wait until you see what she's created in our Mountainview Room and atrium." His praise sounds genuine, not performative. "Frankly, it's better than the original plan."

Before Miranda can respond, a commotion in the driveway announces the arrival of the bride and her parents. Charlene Morton emerges from a white Range Rover; her designer sunglasses pushed into expertly highlighted hair as she surveys her wedding destination.

"Show time." I murmur, moving forward to greet them.

The next few hours blur into a choreographed dance of introductions, tours, and reassurances. I guide the Mortons through the revised venues, emphasizing the intimate spaces' exclusive atmosphere, the glass-domed atrium's magical quality, and the stunning mountain views that frame every aspect of their event. Lucas follows, smoothly adding historical context and answering logistical questions that arise.

To my relief, Charlene's initial skepticism transforms into enthusiasm as she envisions her ceremony beneath the star-filled dome.

"It's like something from a fairy tale." She spins slowly in the circular space adorned with trailing greenery and twinkling lights.

Her mother appears less convinced, examining every detail carefully. "These flowers aren't exactly what we discussed, Amelia."

"The original varieties couldn't be sourced due to the storm." I maintain my professional smile. "Our floral designer selected these premium alternatives specifically to enhance the intimate atmosphere of the new space."

"I'm not sure—"

"Mom, I love them." Charlene interrupts, running fingers over delicate petals. "They're better than what we planned. More romantic."

I catch Lucas's eye across the room, his slight nod acknowledging our narrow escape. One crisis averted, dozens more to navigate before the wedding tomorrow.

"The atrium is acceptable." Miranda materializes at my elbow as the Mortons move to inspect the reception space, voice low. "Though I question your decision to change the ceremony structure completely."

"The glass dome offers a unique experience impossible in the original space." I keep my tone confident despite the knot forming in my stomach. "The client is delighted."

"For now." Her smile doesn't reach her eyes. "But if anything—anything at all—goes wrong tomorrow, that delight will evaporate."

Lucas approaches before I can respond, expertly drawing Miranda into a conversation about the resort's features. I use the moment to escape, retreating to the kitchen to check on the final menu preparations.

The catering team works efficiently under Chef Morgan's direction. The infamous chocolate soufflé sits in test form on a side counter, looking impossibly perfect after our many failed attempts. I'm examining it when a deep voice behind me makes me jump.

"That's a serious expression for a dessert."

I turn to find a tall man in an expensive suit, his easy smile suggesting confidence born of privilege.

"Just ensuring everything meets expectations."

"Ah, you must be the famous Amelia." He extends a hand. "Brock Sterling, best man and childhood friend of our lovely bride."

"Pleasure to meet you." I shake his hand, noting his appraising gaze.

"I've heard you've been working miracles up here." His casual tone carries an undercurrent of curiosity. "Quite impressive under the circumstances."

"It's been a team effort." I glance at my watch, anxious to continue my rounds. "If you'll excuse me, I need to—"

"Is that Brock Sterling I hear terrorizing my staff?" Lucas enters the kitchen, crossing to clap the man on the shoulder casually.

"Lucas Reid. I thought the name of this place sounded familiar. You sly bastard—you actually did it." Recognition lights Brock's face.

"Did what?" Lucas accepts the other man's enthusiastic handshake, smile guarded.

"Escaped the corporate meat grinder for mountain living." Brock laughs. "Last I saw you; you were dismantling the Harrington hotel chain piece by piece, making enemies and millions in equal measure."

Something uncomfortable twists in my stomach at this reminder of Lucas's corporate past—a side of him I've glimpsed but not fully confronted.

"That was another lifetime ago." Lucas's expression remains pleasant, though I notice tension in his shoulders.

"Oh come on, don't be modest." Brock turns to me, eyes

bright with mischief. "This man was the most ruthless acquisitions specialist in the business. 'The Executioner,' they called him. Could find a company's weakness and exploit it before the CEO finished his morning coffee."

"Brock exaggerates." Lucas's jaw tightens imperceptibly.

"Do I?" Brock raises an eyebrow. "Tell that to the Thompson family. Three generations building a respectable hotel business, and you dismantled it in what, six weeks?"

An uncomfortable silence falls between them. I watch Lucas's expression, searching for signs of the corporate shark beneath the mountain innkeeper.

"People change, Brock." Lucas's voice remains calm but carries a warning edge. "Or at least, some of us do."

The subtle jab hits its mark. Brock's smile falters before he forces a laugh. "Fair enough. However, I'm surprised to find you running a place like this instead of owning it. Last I heard, you were buying properties, not preserving them."

"I own it." Lucas's correction comes swiftly and firmly. "And I'm preserving it because some things deserve to be protected, not dismantled for parts."

The conversation shifts to safer territory—mutual acquaintances, the upcoming wedding, and Brock's latest business ventures. I excuse myself to continue my preparations, but Lucas's words echo in my mind. Some things deserve to be protected. The sentiment reveals more about his transformation than any explanation he's offered before.

The rehearsal dinner unfolds in the smaller dining room, which our team has transformed into an elegant alpine retreat. Candles flicker in rustic lanterns, casting warm light across linen-draped tables adorned with arrangements of winter berries and evergreens. The Morton party fills the space with conversation and laughter that grows louder as the wine flows freely.

I remain on the periphery, watchful for potential issues,

and coordinate with staff through discreet signals and quiet instructions. Lucas moves among the guests, the consummate host, though he maintains a professional distance from me whenever Miranda's gaze falls our way.

The crisis, when it comes, arrives with dessert. As servers present the test version of Grandmother Rose's chocolate soufflé to Charlene and her family, the bride's face crumples in disappointment.

"This isn't right." She pokes at the delicate dessert with her spoon. "The texture is all wrong. Grandma's was lighter, almost cloud-like."

"I thought you said you could recreate the recipe precisely." Her mother's expression sharpens.

"Madame, I assure you this soufflé is technically perfect." Chef Morgan emerges from the kitchen, affronted by the criticism.

"Perfect but wrong." Charlene pushes the plate away, tears threatening. "It was the one thing I wanted—something of Grandma's at my wedding."

"Chef, could it be the folding technique? The recipe mentioned a specific method." I step forward, my mind racing for solutions.

Lucas appears at my side, seamlessly joining the problem-solving. "What if we reduce the cooking time slightly? That might create the lighter texture Charlene remembers."

Together, we herd the increasingly agitated chef back to the kitchen while Lucas smoothly directs the servers to offer alternative desserts to the guests. In the relative privacy of the kitchen, we huddle over the recipe, analyzing each step for potential adjustments.

"We need more egg whites." I point to the ingredient list. "And a gentler fold, just like Lucas showed me during our test batches."

"That would defy classical technique—" Chef Morgan bristles.

"This isn't about classical technique." Lucas cuts in, voice firm but not unkind. "It's about recreating a specific memory for our bride. A grandmother's recipe carries emotional weight beyond culinary precision."

The chef studies us both, professional pride warring with the reality of the situation. Finally, he sighs. "Very well. We will try your adjustments for tomorrow's service."

"Thank you, Chef." Lucas's relief is palpable. "Let's prepare a small test batch tonight so Charlene can approve the changes."

As the kitchen team assembles ingredients, Lucas pulls me toward the large pantry, ostensibly to search for the specific vanilla mentioned in the recipe. The moment the door swings shut behind us, he exhales heavily.

"That was close." He runs a hand through his hair. "For a moment, I thought we might have a mutiny on our hands."

"Chef Morgan's ego is almost as big as his talent." I scan the shelves for the elusive vanilla, trying to ignore how small the space feels with Lucas's tall frame blocking the exit. "But you handled him perfectly."

"We handled him perfectly." He steps closer to help with the search. "Your instinct about the folding technique was exactly right."

I'm acutely aware of his proximity in the confined space, surrounded by the rich scents of spices and herbs. We haven't been truly alone since the staff arrived and haven't had a moment to address the question that hung between us this morning.

"Lucas." His name emerges softer than intended. "About what happens after the wedding—"

"I've been thinking about that." He turns to face me, close

enough that I can feel the warmth radiating from his body. "These past days have been... unexpected."

The understatement pulls a small laugh from me. "That's one way to put it."

"I don't want it to end with the wedding." His hand rises, fingers brushing a strand of hair from my face.

The simple admission sends heat cascading through me. Before I can respond, his phone buzzes insistently in his pocket. He ignores it, eyes holding mine in the dim pantry light.

"We should talk about this." My voice sounds strained even to my ears. "Really talk, not just—"

"I know." His hand cups my cheek, thumb tracing my lower lip in a gesture that short-circuits logical thought. "Tonight, after the rehearsal ends."

The phone buzzes again, more urgently. He checks the screen reluctantly. "It's the front desk. I need to take this."

He steps away, answering the call while I try to compose myself. My pulse thrums with everything unspoken between us. When the pantry door opens again, I expect Lucas but find Miranda instead, her expression unreadable.

"There you are." She steps inside, closing the door behind her. "We need to talk, away from clients and... distractions."

Her pointed tone makes it clear what—or who—she considers a distraction. I straighten, professional mask sliding back into place. "Is there a problem with the arrangements?"

"Not with the wedding." She studies me carefully. "But potentially with your judgment."

"Meaning?" I match her directness, refusing to be intimidated.

"Meaning I've noticed your... closeness with the resort owner." Her eyebrows lift slightly. "A professional relationship that appears to have evolved during your isolation here."

Heat rises to my cheeks despite my efforts to remain

impassive. "Lucas and I have worked closely to salvage this event under extraordinary circumstances."

"Indeed." Her smile lacks warmth. "So closely that I wonder if your decision-making remains objective."

"Every decision I've made has been in the client's best interest." I keep my voice level, though indignation burns beneath my calm exterior. "The results speak for themselves."

"They do." She concedes with a slight nod. "Which is why the board has approved your promotion to head our new Paris office, effective immediately after this wedding concludes."

The news should elicit joy, triumph, and validation. Instead, it lands like a stone in the pit of my stomach.

"Paris? Immediately?"

"Amelia... It's the opportunity you've been working toward for years." Miranda watches my reaction carefully. "Complete creative control, doubled salary, an apartment in the 7th arrondissement. Everything you've wanted."

Everything I thought I wanted. Now, I want something more.

"I'm honored by the offer." I buy time to process. "When would I need to give my decision?"

"Decision?" Her laughter holds genuine surprise. "Amelia, this isn't an offer to consider. It's a promotion to accept. Unless..." Her gaze sharpens. "Unless something—or someone —has changed your career aspirations."

The implication hangs between us, challenge and warning intertwined. Before I can respond, the pantry door opens again, revealing a kitchen assistant searching for supplies.

"Excuse me." He mumbles, embarrassed to have inter-rupted what appears to be a private conversation.

"Think carefully about what you've worked for and what you're willing to sacrifice for a... vacation romance." Miranda steps back, professional smile firmly in place. She exits, leaving me alone with thoughts suddenly thrown into chaos.

Paris. The culmination of years of sacrifice and perfectionism. The validation I've sought since joining Elite Events. The proof that I'm exceptional, irreplaceable, and worthy.

Yet, as I return to the rehearsal dinner, watching Lucas charm the wedding party genuinely, something tugs beneath my breastbone—an unfamiliar ache that has nothing to do with career ambition and everything to do with connection, belonging, and the unexpected discovery that perfection might look different than I've always imagined.

The remainder of the evening passes in a blur of conflicting emotions. I perform my duties automatically while my mind grapples with impossible choices. Every time Lucas catches my eye across the room, the pressure in my chest intensifies.

Later, alone in the quiet of Lucas's cabin—he remained at the lodge to handle last-minute guest concerns—I stand at the window, watching moonlight transform snow-covered pines into silver sculptures.

Paris waits with everything I've worked toward. A dazzling future built on ambition and excellence.

But here, in this place, something else has taken root—something unplanned, imperfect, and terrifying. Something that makes the thought of leaving feel like losing a piece of myself I've only just discovered.

For the first time in my meticulously organized life, I have no contingency plan.

CHAPTER 14

TRUE VOWS

DAWN BREAKS OVER ANGEL'S PEAK IN WATERCOLOR strokes of pink and gold. I've been awake for hours, reviewing checklists and contingency plans until the words blur together.

The wedding day has arrived—the culmination of months of planning, days of crisis management, and countless moments of unexpected connection with the resort owner who has upended my carefully structured world.

I haven't seen Lucas since the rehearsal dinner. He sent a text late last night—an apology for being caught up with last-minute lodge issues and a promise to connect in the morning. I drafted a dozen responses, each attempting to convey the complicated tangle of emotions churning inside me before settling on a simple acknowledgment.

We both have jobs to do. Personal revelations will have to wait.

The bridal suite bustles with activity when I arrive. Makeup artists and hair stylists orbit Charlene like planets around a sun while bridesmaids in matching silk robes snap photos and sip mimosas. The bride herself sits eerily calm at the center of the chaos, meeting my eyes in the mirror as I enter.

"Amelia." She smiles, genuine warmth replacing her usual entitled demeanor. "Everything looks magical. The flowers, the atrium—it's better than I ever imagined."

Her sincerity catches me off guard. "I'm glad you're pleased. How are you feeling?"

"Strangely peaceful." She accepts a mimosa from a hovering bridesmaid. "After all the changes and challenges, I realized something important: the perfect wedding isn't about perfect details. It's about marrying the right person in a place that feels special."

The simple wisdom lands unexpectedly. I manage a smile, though her words echo uncomfortably against the tangle of my thoughts about perfection and priorities.

"We still have a few hours before the ceremony." I check my watch, redirecting to safer territory. "I'll make sure everything is on schedule."

The morning unfolds in a whirlwind of final preparations. Florists make last-minute adjustments to the atrium's floral archway. Audio technicians test sound levels for the string quartet. Catering staff transform the Mountainview Room into a reception worthy of society pages.

I'm inspecting the cake placement when the first crisis hits —a frantic call from the makeup artist. The mother of the bride has decided she hates her look and is demanding a complete restart, throwing off the entire preparation timeline.

The second crisis emerges before I can address the first. One of the quartet musicians has food poisoning, leaving them without a cellist for the ceremony music.

The third crisis arrives via text from the best man: the groom has lost the wedding rings.

Breathe, I remind myself, ducking into a quiet alcove.

Crises are just problems waiting for solutions. I've handled worse with fewer resources. Yet the pressure of perfection weighs heavier today, with Miranda's watchful gaze and the Paris position hanging in the balance—not to mention my confusion about what I want.

"There you are." Lucas's voice pulls me from spiraling thoughts.

He stands in the hallway, devastatingly handsome in a charcoal suit that emphasizes the breadth of his shoulders and the lean strength of his frame. For a moment, all the professional chaos recedes, replaced by the simpler chaos of my feelings for this complicated man.

"Crisis central." I gesture to my phone, where messages continue to arrive. "Standard wedding day emergencies."

"Anything I can help with?" He steps closer, careful professionalism in his posture despite the warmth in his eyes.

I hesitate only briefly before dividing the list. "Can you track down the rings? The best man says Brock last had them during the poker game last night."

"Consider it handled." His confidence steadies me. "What else?"

"We need a cellist. One of the quartet is sick."

He thinks for a moment, then nods. "My maintenance manager, Paul, played professionally before moving to the mountains. I'll call him."

"Thank you." Relief flutters through me. "I'll handle the mother-of-the-bride makeup crisis."

We separate, each tackling our assigned problems. The pattern continues throughout the morning—one of us identifying an issue, the other stepping in with a solution, moving in harmony without the need for extensive communication.

When the florist discovers damage to key ceremony arrangements, Lucas produces replacement blooms from the resort's greenhouse. When a groomsman's tuxedo arrives with the wrong size pants, I find the lodge's tailor for emergency alterations.

By the time guests arrive for the ceremony, every crisis has been addressed, every detail perfected. I stand at the entrance to the atrium, directing ushers and greeting important attendees, when Miranda appears at my side.

"Impressive recovery." She surveys the transformed space grudgingly.

"Everything is proceeding exactly as planned." I maintain professional confidence despite the flutter of uncertainty her presence triggers. "The revised venue has enhanced the experience."

Her gaze shifts to where Lucas stands across the room, conversing easily with the father of the bride. "And your decision about Paris? Have you come to your senses?"

"I'll give you my answer after the wedding." The question twists uncomfortably.

"Make sure it's the right one." She smooths her already impeccable jacket. "Opportunities like this don't come twice."

She glides away to schmooze with potential clients among the guest list, leaving me with the weight of impending choices.

Before I can dwell on it further, the coordinator signals that it's time to begin. I usher the final guests to their seats, ensure the bride is in position with her father, and cue the musicians to begin.

The ceremony unfolds breathtakingly. Winter sunshine streams through the glass dome, casting the atrium in ethereal light that blesses the proceedings.

Charlene moves down the aisle, transformed not just by her exquisite gown but by the genuine joy that radiates from within. Guests gasp as they absorb the magical setting—the circular space embraced by cascading flowers and twinkling lights. The mountains, visible beyond the glass, create the impression of a ceremony suspended between heaven and earth.

At the back of the room, I survey my creation satisfyingly, tinged with something more personal. This is more than another successful event. This transformation—born of crisis, shaped by necessity, and executed against impossible odds—represents something new in my perfectionist approach.

"You've created something extraordinary here." Lucas appears beside me as vows are exchanged, his presence both comforting and unsettling. His voice comes soft enough that only I can hear, gaze still on the ceremony. "Not just beautiful, but meaningful."

The simple compliment warms me more than elaborate praise might have. "We did. Together."

His hand finds mine between us, hidden from observers, fingers intertwining intimately. "I've been thinking about what you said—about trust being difficult for you."

I tense slightly, uncertain where this conversation is heading while surrounded by wedding guests. "This isn't the time—"

"I know. But I need you to know something." His thumb traces circles against my palm, sending shivers up my arm. "I've never worked with anyone the way I work with you. Never trusted anyone with something as important as this place."

The weight of his words settles in my chest alongside the knowledge of the opportunity waiting in Paris. Before I can respond, the ceremony concludes enthusiastically, the newly married couple beaming as they process back down the aisle.

The moment for personal confessions evaporates as we seamlessly transition to our professional roles once more, directing the flow of guests toward the reception.

The Mountainview Room glitters with winter elegance—tables adorned with crystal and silver, centerpieces of white blooms, and evergreen boughs catching the light from suspended candles and twinkling fairy lights.

Snow falls gently beyond the floor-to-ceiling windows, nature's perfect backdrop to our carefully crafted interior. Guests exclaim over the transformation, many commenting that the weather emergency has resulted in a more intimate, magical setting than the original plan.

"You've outdone yourself." Charlene's father approaches as I supervise the transition from cocktail hour to dinner service. "When they told me we were moving the reception, I expected disaster. This is... exceptional."

"Thank you, Mr. Morton." I accept his praise professionally. "The resort provided the perfect canvas."

"And the owner seems equally exceptional." His gaze shifts meaningfully to where Lucas chats with guests across the room. "You two make quite the team. Haven't seen coordination like that since my days in special forces."

Before I can formulate a properly neutral response, his wife calls him away, leaving me with the uncomfortable awareness that our connection—whatever it is—has become noticeable to others.

I throw myself into final dinner preparations, maintaining distance from Lucas as we perform our roles in separate orbits.

The evening progresses in the comfortable rhythm of a well-executed event. Dinner service unfolds flawlessly. The revised menu draws appreciative murmurs. Grandmother's chocolate soufflé—perfected after our crisis intervention—brings tears to Charlene's eyes, which is exactly the emotional reaction we'd hoped for.

Toasts elicit both laughter and sentimental sighs. The band strikes the perfect balance between elegant background music and danceable energy.

I check the dessert station when the best man takes the microphone. His voice fills the room.

"Ladies and gentlemen, before we continue the celebration, the bride and groom have a special request." Brock grins, clearly enjoying whatever is coming. "They'd like to acknowledge the dream team that made this magical wedding possible despite impossible circumstances—Amelia Hayes and Lucas Reid!"

Surprised applause fills the room as a spotlight finds me at the dessert station. Lucas appears equally startled on the opposite side of the room. His eyes find mine across the distance.

"And." Brock continues mischievously. "They've requested that these two extraordinary individuals share a dance with them."

Heat rises to my cheeks as Lucas approaches, offering his hand with a slight shrug that says, We have little choice.

The band transitions to a slow melody as we move to the center of the floor. His hand settles at my waist carefully despite the electric awareness that sparks between us.

"Ambushed." His whisper carries humor as we begin to move to the music. "Though I can't say I mind."

"Very professional." I maintain enough distance to appear appropriate while hyperaware of every point of contact between us—his hand at my waist, mine on his shoulder, our fingers intertwined.

"Professional went out the window days ago, Amelia." His voice drops lower, for my ears only. "Somewhere between blizzards and soufflés and elevator encounters."

The reminder of our more intimate moments sends heat cascading through me. "Lucas, I—"

"I know we need to talk." His eyes hold mine, honest and direct in a way that makes my chest ache. "About whatever this is between us. About what happens after tomorrow."

The music swells around us as we move perfectly together —another example of how naturally we fit together. Our bodies remember steps neither of us consciously leads. I'm acutely aware of guests watching, of Miranda's calculating gaze tracking our every move, of the precipice we stand upon.

"I've been offered Paris." The words escape before I can reconsider, quiet but clear between us. "Running Elite's European division. It's the promotion I've worked toward for years."

"When?" His rhythm falters almost imperceptibly before he recovers.

"Immediately after the wedding concludes." I search his expression for a reaction. "It's a tremendous opportunity."

"It is." His agreement comes without hesitation, though something flickers in his eyes—disappointment, perhaps, or resignation. "When do you leave?"

"I haven't accepted yet."

"Why not?" This surprises him. His hand tightens slightly at my waist. "It's everything you've worked for, isn't it?"

The question echoes my internal struggle. "It was. Before..."

"Before what?" He prompts me when I don't continue.

Before you.

Before us.

Before I discovered that perfection might look different than I've always believed.

The words crowd my throat but remain unspoken as the music draws to a close. Applause surrounds us as we step apart, the moment for confession lost in the social requirements of the reception.

The remainder of the evening passes in a blur of professional obligations. Lucas and I orbit each other cautiously, both aware of unfinished conversations and uncertain futures.

As guests gradually depart and the newlyweds retreat to their suite, we oversee the final breakdown of the venue, directing staff efficiently as always.

"You should get some rest." Lucas appears beside me as I

check the final vendor departure list. "Tomorrow will be another long day."

Tomorrow.

When the bubble bursts completely. When reality reasserts itself in the form of departing guests, returning to normal operations, and decisions about Paris that can no longer be postponed.

"You too." I try for professional detachment despite the weight of everything unsaid between us. "It's been a successful event. The resort will certainly see increased bookings from this exposure."

"Is that what we're doing?" His voice carries quiet challenge. "Pretending this was just a business transaction?"

"Isn't it?" The question emerges more vulnerable than intended.

"You know it isn't." Lucas steps closer, close enough that I can smell the subtle notes of his cologne and see the faint shadow of stubble along his jaw.

"Then what was it?" I meet his gaze directly, needing clarity before I can make impossible choices.

"A beginning." His answer comes without hesitation. "Or at least, I thought it could be."

"Lucas, I—" The simple honesty in his expression steals my breath.

"You don't need to decide anything tonight." He reaches out, tucking a strand of hair behind my ear gently. "Just promise me one thing."

"What?"

"Don't decide about Paris based solely on your career." His fingers linger against my cheek. "Make it based on what makes you happy."

The request lands like a stone in still water, ripples spreading outward through everything I've believed about success and fulfillment. What makes me happy? The question is simultaneously simple and profoundly disorienting.

"I should go." I step back, needing distance to think clearly. "Early morning tomorrow."

He nods, accepting my retreat reluctantly. "Goodnight, Amelia."

I make it halfway to the door before turning back. "For what it's worth, these past days with you... they've changed how I see things. How I see myself."

"For what it's worth." He echoes. "They've been the most challenging and rewarding days I've had since taking over this place. Regardless of what you decide about Paris."

We stand separated by the empty reception room, the space between us filled with possibility and uncertainty. Tomorrow looms with its demands for decisions and good-byes, for choosing between the career I've built and something entirely unexpected that's taken root in this mountain sanctuary.

CHAPTER 15

CREATIVE SOLUTIONS

MORNING LIGHT FILTERS THROUGH THE GUEST room window, falling across the small suitcase open on the bed. I fold another sweater, adding it to the meager collection of belongings I'll take when I leave Angel's Peak.

The wedding concluded in picture-perfect glory yesterday, the Mortons departing for their honeymoon with effusive praise for both the resort and my crisis management skills. Most guests have already checked out, returning to their regular lives with photos and memories of a mountain fairytale.

Only I remain, caught between worlds—the career waiting in Paris and the unexpected connection forged in this snow-covered haven.

A knock at the door interrupts my packing. I open it to find Miranda dressed in a sleek traveling suit, her designer luggage waiting in the hallway behind her.

"My car leaves in thirty minutes." She steps inside without invitation, assessing my half-packed suitcase critically. "I need your answer about Paris before I go."

No preamble.

No congratulations on the wedding's success.

Just the direct pressure I've come to expect from her over the years.

"I'm still considering the offer." I close the door, steeling myself for the confrontation brewing in her narrowed gaze.

"Considering?" Disbelief colors her tone. "Amelia, this is the opportunity you've worked toward since you joined Elite. The cornerstone of the five-year plan you presented in your last performance review."

"I'm aware." I move to the window, buying time as I gaze at the mountains bathed in morning light. "It's just a significant life change to commit to immediately."

Miranda's reflection appears beside mine in the glass, her expression a mixture of confusion and calculation. "This isn't like you. You've always been decisive, ambitious."

"I'm still those things." I turn to face her directly. "But perhaps my ambitions are evolving."

"This is about him. The resort owner." Understanding dawns in her eyes.

"This is about me." The correction comes firmly. "About what I want for my future."

"And suddenly that's unclear?" Her eyebrows lift skeptically. "After years of single-minded focus on reaching the top of the industry?"

The question deserves honest consideration. I take a moment before answering, finding clarity even as I speak.

"What if reaching the top looks different than I imagined? What if there's a way to achieve success that includes personal fulfillment?"

"Personal fulfillment." She repeats the words as if they're in a foreign language. "Amelia, this business isn't compatible with sentimentality. You've always understood that."

"I'm not being sentimental." I gesture toward the window,

toward the resort beyond. "I'm being strategic. There are opportunities here I hadn't considered."

"I need an answer by this evening. The board expects confirmation of your acceptance so they can announce the appointment at next week's shareholders meeting." Miranda studies me calculatingly.

"You'll have my decision." I match her professional tone, refusing to be rushed despite the pressure.

After she leaves, I return to packing with less certainty than before. My phone buzzes with a text from Lucas: Coffee in the dining room when you're ready. No rush.

The casual message belies the weight of decisions hanging between us. We haven't spoken privately since our conversation after the reception, both swept up in the final wedding responsibilities and guest departures.

The dining room is nearly empty when I arrive. Most wedding guests have already departed. Lucas sits at a corner table with two steaming mugs, looking up with a smile that does unreasonable things to my pulse.

"Successful wedding." He pushes a cup toward me as I sit across from him. "The Mortons couldn't stop raving."

"Everything came together perfectly." I warm my hands around the mug, studying him over the rim. He looks tired but satisfied, the same way I feel—the particular exhaustion that follows a job well done.

"Charlene and Jason stopped by my office before leaving." He leans back in his chair, the morning light accentuating the strong lines of his jaw. "They want to book their first-anniversary celebration here. Said the resort felt magical."

Pride warms me, both professionally and personally. "We did create something special."

"We did." His gaze holds mine, the simple agreement laden with meaning beyond the wedding's success.

The moment stretches between us, filled with everything

yet unspoken. Finally, I break the silence. "Miranda wants my answer about Paris by this evening."

Something flickers across his expression—perhaps resignation or carefully controlled disappointment. "And have you decided?"

"I'm still weighing options." I trace the rim of my mug, organizing my thoughts. "It's the opportunity I've worked toward for years."

"But?" He prompts gently when I don't continue.

"But I'm not the same person who set those goals." The admission comes easier than expected. "These past days have shown me different possibilities, different definitions of success."

Hope brightens his eyes before he carefully masks it. "Whatever you decide, I want you to know that what happened here—between us—it wasn't just circumstance or isolation."

The simple honesty in his voice settles something restless inside me. Before I can respond, his phone buzzes with a message that draws his attention away.

"The photography team just delivered the wedding portfolio." He glances up apologetically. "I need to review it before sending to the Mortons. Would you like to join me?"

We relocate to his office, a surprisingly cozy space with large windows overlooking the mountains and comfortable leather furniture that invites lingering rather than efficiency. His large monitor displays the wedding photos, a visual record of our collaborative creation.

The images are stunning—Charlene radiant beneath the glass dome, surrounded by flowers and light; guests mingling in the transformed Mountainview Room; details of table settings and food presentations captured artistically. Each photo reveals layers of thought and care, the successful marriage of my planning and Lucas's venue.

"These are exceptional." I lean closer to the screen, profes-sional satisfaction mingling with personal pride. "The atrium especially photographs like a dream."

"It could be the cornerstone of a dedicated wedding program." Lucas flips to another series of images. "We've never marketed specifically for weddings before, but after this success..."

His casual observation triggers something in my mind—a cascade of possibilities unfolding like dominoes. The resort's unique features. The relatively untapped market for luxury mountain weddings. The perfect marriage of his venue and my expertise.

"You could become the premier wedding destination in the region." The idea gains momentum as I speak it aloud. "The atrium alone offers something no other venue can match."

"You're seeing something." Lucas watches me intensely as I pace his office, thoughts crystallizing into vision.

"Potential." I turn to him, my excitement building. "This resort has untapped potential in the luxury wedding market. The intimate scale, the unique spaces, the exclusivity of loca-tion—they're all perfect selling points for high-end events."

"Go on." His smile widens as he follows my reasoning.

"You'd need a dedicated wedding program. Specialized packages. Seasonal offerings. Strategic partnerships with premier vendors." Ideas flow faster than I can articulate them. My professional instincts engage with a familiar challenge in a new context. "And incredible marketing—not just photos but a complete brand story about mountain romance and exclu-sive experiences."

"Sounds like a business plan in the making." He leans against his desk, watching me admiringly. "One that would require experienced leadership."

The implication hangs between us, unspoken but clear.

Before I can respond, his phone rings—another resort matter requiring immediate attention.

"I need to handle this." He gestures apologetically toward the door. "Feel free to keep reviewing the photos. We can continue this conversation later?"

After he leaves, I remain in his office, scrolling through wedding images while my mind races with expanding possibilities. What began as casual observation has ignited something I recognize from my earliest days at Elite—the thrill of identifying untapped potential, of envisioning something extraordinary where others see merely adequate.

I open a blank document on Lucas's computer and begin typing, capturing ideas before they evaporate. Initial market analysis. Competitive advantages. Service offerings. Pricing structures. Revenue projections. Hours slip by unnoticed as the outline of a business plan takes shape beneath my fingers.

By late afternoon, I've moved beyond basics to detailed program components—signature wedding packages named after mountain peaks, seasonal specialties leveraging the resort's natural advantages, and exclusive experiences only Angel's Peak can offer. The more I develop the concept, the more convinced I become of its viability.

This isn't just a viable alternative to Paris—it's potentially more fulfilling and more challenging in the ways that matter to me. I'm building something from vision to reality, using my skills to execute others' dreams and create something uniquely mine.

Ours, perhaps, if Lucas sees the same potential.

Darkness falls outside the windows as I refine the document, adding financial projections based on industry standards and my experience with Elite's high-end clientele. When Miranda's message demands my decision, I respond without hesitation: I won't be accepting the Paris position. A formal letter will follow tomorrow.

Relief floods through me as I send the message, followed by certainty that I've made the right choice. Not for Lucas, though he factors into the equation, but for myself—for the vision of success that aligns with who I am now, not who I believed I needed to be.

I save the document, attaching it to an email addressed to Lucas with the subject line: "A Proposition."

In the body, I write simply: Not a business plan yet, but the beginnings of one. I see tremendous potential for the Haven at Angel's Peak in the luxury wedding market. I'd like to discuss how we might develop this together.

My finger hovers over the send button, aware of all this email potentially initiates—a new career direction, a reason to stay, a future intertwined with Lucas's in ways both professional and personal. I take a deep breath, clicking send, committing to this new path.

As I gather my things to return to my room, my phone chimes with a text notification. Lucas's name appears on the screen with a message that sends heat cascading through me: Come to my cabin. Now.

The commanding tone, so different from his previous messages, triggers memories of our earliest encounters—the primal chemistry that preceded deeper connection. I hesitate only briefly before responding: On my way.

CHAPTER 16

THIS IS WHERE WE BEGIN

NIGHT HAS FULLY DESCENDED AS I FOLLOW THE now-familiar path to Lucas's cabin. Lights glow from within, casting warm rectangles on the surrounding snow. When I knock, no one answers, but the door swings open at my touch.

The cabin appears empty, though a fire crackles in the hearth. A folded note with my name written in Lucas's strong hand sits on the kitchen counter. I open it, fingers trembling slightly, my pulse quickening at the simple instruction:

I've read your proposal. We have much to discuss. But first, something more urgent. Follow the path.

Rose petals form a trail across the floor, leading toward the bedroom. As I follow them, my anticipation builds with each step.

I notice subtle changes to the familiar space—candles casting golden light, the scent of sandalwood hanging in the air, soft music playing.

The path ends at the archway to his bedroom, where black silk restraints dangle suggestively from the wooden beam above. Another note waits on a small table beneath them, this one more explicit:

Strip. Kneel. Wait. Put on the blindfold.

Beside the note rests a black silk blindfold, its presence both an invitation and command. Heat pools low in my belly as I recognize the game—his dominance that perfectly complements my need to surrender control.

I remove my clothing piece by piece, folding each item neatly despite the desire coursing through me. The air kisses my bare skin, raising gooseflesh across my arms and breasts. I lift the blindfold, securing it over my eyes before lowering myself to my knees on the soft rug beneath the archway.

Darkness heightens every other sense—the whisper of air against my skin, the distant crackle of the fire, the subtle scent of Lucas's cologne that tells me he's entered the room even before I hear his footsteps.

"Beautiful." His voice comes from behind me, low and appreciative. "You follow instructions well."

"Only yours." The admission emerges breathier than intended.

His hand touches my shoulder, a feather-light contact that sends electricity racing across my skin. "I read your proposal."

That's not what I expect him to say at this moment. "And?"

"It's brilliant." His fingers trace my collarbone, a maddening caress that makes concentration difficult. "Like you."

"You want to discuss business now?" I can't keep the incredulity from my voice, though it dissolves into a gasp as his hand slides lower.

"No." The word carries a smile I can hear rather than see. "I want to celebrate that you're not going to Paris."

My breath catches. "How did you—"

"Miranda was quite vocal about your 'career suicide' in the lobby earlier." His hand tangles in my hair, tilting my head back gently but firmly. "Something about choosing a 'mountain fling' over the opportunity of a lifetime."

"That's not why I declined." It's important that he understand this, even as his proximity makes coherent thought challenging. "I declined because I found something better. A vision I believe in."

"I know." His lips brush my ear, sending shivers down my spine. "That's what makes you extraordinary. Your ability to see possibilities others miss."

His praise warms me in ways distinct from, but complementary to, the physical desire building between us. His hand traces down my back, following the curve of my spine deliberately.

"Now." His voice drops lower, taking on the commanding edge that melts my resistance. "Are you ready to surrender your brilliant mind for a while? To let go completely?"

"Yes." The word emerges without hesitation.

"Good girl." He reaches up, and I hear the soft clink of the restraints being adjusted. "Hands above your head."

I comply, anticipation tightening my muscles as the silk wraps around first one wrist and then the other. Not uncomfortably tight—I could escape if I wished—but secure enough to reinforce the surrender of control.

"Tell me if anything feels wrong." His voice softens momentarily, the caretaking dominant checking my comfort. "Your safe word?"

"Chardonnay."

"Perfect." His approval sends warmth coursing through me as his hands resume their exploration, tracing patterns across my skin that make me arch toward his touch. "Now, about this business proposal of yours..."

I laugh despite the intensity of the moment. "Seriously?"

"I take business very seriously, Ms. Hayes." His tone carries mock severity, belied by how his hands continue their maddening journey across my body. "Particularly partnerships that hold such... promising potential."

His fingers find the sensitive skin of my inner thigh, drawing ever closer to where I ache for his touch without quite delivering relief. "I think we should negotiate terms, don't you?"

Understanding dawns through the haze of desire. This is his way of confirming my commitment—to staying and building something together, both professionally and personally.

"What terms did you have in mind?" My voice breaks as his touch grows bolder.

His lips brush against my shoulder, then move toward my neck in a trail of feather-light kisses. "Exclusivity, for one."

"Granted." The word emerges as a gasp when his teeth graze my pulse point.

"Long-term investment." His hand slides around to my stomach, fingers splayed possessively against my skin. "I don't enter partnerships lightly, Amelia."

"Neither do I." I strain against the restraints, seeking closer contact with his body behind mine.

"Complete transparency." His voice drops to a whisper directly against my ear. "No more masks between us. Just truth."

The request penetrates deeper than physical desire, touching the core of what's grown between us these past days —the recognition of someone who sees beyond my carefully constructed façade to the woman beneath.

His hands still, a sudden seriousness in his posture that I can sense even without seeing him. The air shifts. Thickens. A current ripples between us—charged and waiting.

"There's one more thing I need."

"What?" My voice emerges breathless, suspended in the moment, stretched thin over the drumbeat of my pulse.

"Your obedience. The ability to command you. Control you." His fingers trace my jawline deliberately, leaving fire in their wake. "And when necessary... to punish you."

The words slam into me like a storm surge—unyielding and impossible to run from.

Heat floods me. Not shame—never that—but a heady, overwhelming rush of relief and desire. Like I've been holding my breath for days, maybe my whole life, and he's finally offering me air.

This is what I've been craving.

Not a game. Not a scene built on safe words and rehearsed roles.

But something real.

A man powerful enough to subdue me completely. Not just in the bedroom, but in the quiet, gritty spaces where control means something. Where obedience isn't negotiated—it's expected. Where punishment isn't fantasy—it's structure.

Earned. Delivered. Felt.

I've always wanted to surrender like that. To be taken—utterly, unapologetically—and held to it. No matter how loud I beg. No matter how much I shake.

I tilt my face toward the sound of his voice. My lips part. And when I speak, it's not a plea.

It's a vow.

"I want to be everything you need me to be." I whisper. "You have me... all of me."

A beat of silence. Then—

His inhale sharpens, ragged and unsteady.

"Does this mean..." I swallow hard. "The line in the sand is gone?"

"It's been erased." His voice is gravel and heat when it finally comes. A pause, electric. "I plan to redraw everything we are from the ground up."

I feel it in my bones—this is more than dominance. It's

devotion, forged through fire and withheld pleasure and every boundary we've broken together.

"Yes." The word emerges with surprising certainty. "I want that."

His breath shudders out—a release of something he's held tight for too long. "You're sure?"

"I've never been more certain of anything."

"Then say it clearly." His eyes search mine, unblinking.

"I give you the right to command, control, and punish me as you see fit." I swallow and say the rest. "To master me."

His arm wraps around my waist, pulling me flush against the hard line of his body.

"Are you ready to burn for me, Amelia?" He asks, voice low and dangerous. "To take everything I've been holding back?"

"Yes." I whisper.

"Then, in addition to your previous punishment..." His mouth brushes my ear. His hand slips between my thighs, fingers grazing where I'm already soaked for him. "You'll take ten strikes for each night I slept alone. Each night I couldn't fuck you because I was holding the line."

I gasp—sharp, electric.

"That's four nights, sweetheart." His lips curl against my neck. "Forty strikes. Forty reminders that control has consequences... and so does teasing a man trained to command."

He pauses, and I feel him still—completely still—as if the weight of this moment just slammed into him, too.

"My belt." He says, voice low and rough. "Are you okay with that?"

"Y-yes." The word leaves me shakily. "I'm okay with however you choose to punish me."

A beat.

"Whatever I choose?" There's something in his tone now —something quieter. Not doubt, but awe.

I nod, blindfolded, exposed, trembling not from fear but from the weight of what I'm giving him.

"I give up the right to choose." My voice cracks. "That is yours now."

"Fuck." His breath hitches. His hand clenches on my hip. It's whispered—barely a word, more a revelation. "Do you know what you've just done to me?"

I shake my head. I don't speak. I don't have to.

"I've never had this." His voice vibrates at my back, more confession than command now. "A woman willing to give it all. Not pretend. Not negotiated roles. Not something we can close like a book when we're done playing."

He exhales once, low and deliberate. The air feels charged, like a storm about to break.

"If that's true..." His voice deepens, dark and full of promise. "If you're giving me all of you... then I'm going to take it all."

His hand slides around my throat—not squeezing, just resting there. A possessive touch. A warning. A vow.

"Not just in bed. Not just when you're stripped bare and begging." His lips hover near mine, heat pouring off him like fire restrained by steel. "I'm going to own every part of you. Every look. Every breath. Every choice."

He pauses.

"You have one chance to walk away. Say the word, and I'll give you control again."

The silence pulses like a heartbeat. My breath shakes. But not from fear.

I lift my chin, blindfolded but unflinching.

"I want you in control. I want to feel it. Every second. Every rule. Every consequence." I swallow, pulse thundering. "I want to be yours in every way."

"You're not going to survive me." His groan is guttural—pain and hunger twisted together.

"I don't want to." I whisper.

"Good." His grip on my throat tightens just enough to make me gasp. His mouth brushes mine—barely a kiss, just a promise. "Then we begin."

His mouth claims mine in a kiss that contains multitudes —desire and tenderness, possession and promise. As his hands continue their deliberate exploration of my body, building pleasure skillfully, I surrender completely, trusting him to lead me into the uncharted territory we've discovered together.

Whatever we're building—both the business venture taking shape in my mind and the relationship evolving between us—begins here, in this perfect moment of mutual surrender and shared vision.

A whimper escapes me, but he's not done.

"One more thing." He says, his voice dark silk. "You don't get to come."

I stiffen. "Lucas—"

"No. You teased. You denied. You tempted me again and again, knowing I wouldn't touch you." His hand tightens at my waist. "Now you get to suffer."

He kisses the corner of my mouth.

"For every night you left me hard and aching, you'll take ten strikes..." His thumb grazes my clit—just once—then vanishes.

"...and you'll have no release."

"No..."

"You will ache for me, Amelia. Just as I ached for you." His breath burns against my throat. "And if you beg me to stop, we begin again."

For the next four nights, I burn for him. I ache for him. And I wouldn't want it any other way.

I came to Angel's Peak chasing perfection, armed with color-coded binders and contingency plans. Instead, I found something I never knew I was searching for—peace in surrender, strength in vulnerability, and a man who gives me the structure I need to thrive.

I found the love of a lifetime.

And this? This is just the beginning.

Love the heat in Angel's Peak?

If you're enjoying all the steamy, small-town instalove stories this mountain town has to offer, you're going to fall hard for *Matched with the Small Town Chef.*

This next swoon-worthy romance serves up spice, sweetness, and a hero who knows exactly what he wants—*her.*

🍲 Grab your apron...and your fan. Things are about to get delicious.

➡️ Click here to dive into *Matched with the Small Town Chef!*

CHAPTER 17

EPOLOGUE: FULL CIRCLE

SNOW DRIFTS LAZILY PAST THE ATRIUM'S GLASS dome, creating the perfect backdrop for the anniversary celebration below. I adjust a centerpiece on the head table, my expanded belly making the simple task more challenging than it was a few months ago.

"Stop fussing." Lucas appears at my side, one hand settling protectively over the curve where our daughter grows. "Everything is perfect."

"The florist used ivory roses instead of champagne." I gesture toward the offending arrangement. "And the lighting is slightly—"

"Magical." He completes my sentence differently than intended, pressing a kiss to my temple. "Just like it was a year ago when the Mortons got married here."

One year. It seems impossible that only twelve months have passed since I arrived at Angel's Peak, color-coded binder in hand, determined to execute the perfect wedding despite an impending blizzard. That determined event planner wouldn't recognize the woman I've become—co-owner of a thriving wedding venue, expectant mother, and surprisingly content with imperfection when it matters least.

"Mrs. Reid?" A tentative voice interrupts my reflection. Sophia, the young event coordinator I've been mentoring, approaches with a clipboard in hand. "Chef wants to know if we're still doing the champagne toast at seven or moving it earlier?"

"Seven is perfect." I smile at her obvious anxiety, recognizing my younger self in her meticulous attention to detail.

"Also, the photographer asked about group shots before dinner since it might start snowing harder later."

"Tell him yes," Lucas answers before I can, his hand still resting on my belly where our daughter has begun her evening acrobatics. "And Sophia? You're doing great. Breathe."

Her shoulders relax slightly at his reassurance. "Thank you, Mr. Reid."

"Lucas." He corrects easily. "We only use formal titles with difficult clients."

Once she scurries away, I lean against him, grateful for his solid presence. "She reminds me of myself when I started."

"Terrifyingly efficient with a tendency toward perfectionism?" His teasing carries affection. "I see the resemblance."

"I wasn't that bad." At his raised eyebrow, I add, "Okay, I was worse. But I've improved."

"You've evolved." His correction comes gently. "Though I did notice the color-coded nursery binder on your nightstand."

Heat rises to my cheeks. "Some habits die hard."

"And some shouldn't die at all." His voice drops lower, for my ears alone. "Your organizational skills have significant advantages in certain contexts."

The heated look he gives me sends familiar warmth cascading through my body, a reminder of the many ways our professional and personal dynamics have intertwined over the past year. Even eight months pregnant, he still makes me feel desirable with nothing more than a glance.

"Save that thought for later." I straighten as guests begin to filter into the atrium, now our signature ceremony space, following the unexpected success of the Morton wedding. "We have an anniversary to host."

The Haven at Angel's Peak has transformed in the year since I arrived. My business plan—born of crisis and insight—has expanded the resort from a struggling mountain retreat to the region's premier wedding destination.

Bookings extend two years into the future, each event more elaborate than the last, as our reputation spreads through glossy magazine features and social media buzz.

More importantly, Lucas and I have transformed—from adversaries to reluctant allies to partners in every sense. Our relationship deepened from those early days of physical attraction to something built on mutual respect, complementary skills, and the kind of trust that allows both control and surrender when each is needed.

Charlene and Jason Morton arrive in a flurry of designer winter wear and enthusiastic greetings, looking every bit as in love as they did on their wedding day. After her initial shock at discovering I had declined Paris to become Lucas's business partner, Charlene became both a client and a friend, recommending our venue to her extensive social circle.

"Amelia!" She embraces me awkwardly around my protruding stomach. "Look at you, absolutely glowing. When are you due again?"

"Three more weeks." I rest a hand on my belly as the baby delivers a particularly athletic kick. "Though the doctor says first babies often arrive late."

"She'll come exactly when she's ready." Lucas joins us, shaking Jason's hand warmly. "Not a minute before or after."

"Just like her mother." Jason grins. "Always perfectly on schedule."

"Actually." Lucas's eyes meet mine, amused. "I suspect she'll take after both of us—my spontaneity and her mother's determination. A formidable combination."

The celebration unfolds smoothly. Staff move gracefully, anticipating needs before they arise. The string quartet plays softly in the background as guests mingle beneath the glass dome, snowflakes dancing overhead in nature's perfect decoration.

I circulate among attendees, accepting congratulations both on the successful event and my obvious pregnancy. While Lucas handles wine service and conversation charmingly, I slip into the kitchen to ensure dinner preparations proceed according to plan.

"All is well, madame. Return to your guests." Chef Morgan—who eventually became one of my strongest allies after our rocky beginning—oversees the final plating meticulously.

"Everything looks beautiful." I steal a strawberry from a dessert platter, pregnancy cravings overriding professional restraint. "The soufflé?"

"Perfection, as always." His pride is well-earned; Grandmother Rose's chocolate soufflé has become our signature dessert following its success at the Morton wedding. "Light as air, exactly as it should be."

As I turn to leave, a strange sensation ripples across my abdomen, tighter and more focused than the baby's usual movements. I pause, one hand bracing against the counter as I wait for it to pass.

"Amelia?" The chef's concerned voice seems distant as I focus on the unfamiliar feeling.

"I'm fine." The tightness recedes, leaving me slightly breathless. "Just Braxton Hicks contractions. False labor."

By the time I return to the celebration, the moment has passed, filed away as another pregnancy experience to document in the journal Lucas gave me when we first learned about the baby. I rejoin him as he delivers a toast to the anniversary couple, his natural charisma drawing every eye in the room.

"To Charlene and Jason." He raises his glass. "Whose wedding not only launched our business but changed my life in ways I never imagined. Thank you for bringing a blizzard, a broken venue, and most importantly, a certain perfectionist event planner into my world."

Laughter ripples through the gathering as glasses clink. I accept his kiss when he returns to my side, the simple contact still sending electricity through me after a year together.

"Doing okay?" His whisper carries concern as his hand finds the small of my back.

"Perfect." I lean into his touch. "Though your daughter is practicing Olympic gymnastics tonight."

Dinner proceeds flawlessly, conversation flowing as freely as the wine (sparkling cider for me). As dessert concludes—soufflés met with appropriate admiration—another wave of tightness wraps around my midsection, stronger than before. I breathe through it quietly, unwilling to disrupt the celebration for what must still be false labor.

When a third contraction follows twenty minutes later, doubt begins to creep in. I catch Sophia's eye across the room, signaling her to approach.

"I need you to take over for a bit." I keep my voice steady despite the growing certainty that these are not practice contractions. "Make sure the farewell gifts are distributed when the guests depart."

Her eyes widen as understanding dawns. "Is it time? Should I call the doctor? The hospital? Your midwife?"

"Just find Lucas." I manage a reassuring smile despite another contraction building. "Discreetly."

Lucas appears moments later, concern evident in the set of his shoulders, though his expression remains calm for the benefit of nearby guests. "What's happening?"

"I think she's coming." I grip his hand as the contraction peaks. "Three weeks early, naturally. She couldn't possibly adhere to a schedule."

His laugh holds both excitement and anxiety. "Are you sure?"

As if in answer, I feel a distinct pop followed by warm wetness trickling down my legs. "Absolutely certain."

What follows is both terrifying and comical—Lucas maintaining perfect composure while executing the birth plan we'd carefully constructed, me watching helplessly as each element collapses under the reality of a baby determined to arrive on her timeline during a snowstorm in the middle of an event we're hosting.

"The roads are already closing." Lucas relays information from the sheriff as he helps me to our private quarters in the resort's east wing. "The doctor can't get through from town."

"What?" Panic threatens as another contraction grips me. "No, the plan was to deliver with Dr. Blake. It's in the binder!"

"I've already called him. He's on his way, lives just down the mountain." His voice remains steady as he helps me change into comfortable clothes.

"And if he can't make it through?" The reality of our isolated location suddenly feels less charming than concerning.

"Then we do this together, like everything else this past year. I've read all the books and watched all the videos. Our daughter will arrive safely, with or without medical assistance." Lucas kneels before me, taking both my hands in his.

His certainty calms me despite the increasingly painful contractions. "This wasn't the plan."

"No." He agrees, helping me onto our bed. "It's better. A perfect callback to how we began—trapped by snow, forced to adapt, creating something beautiful from unexpected circumstances."

As labor progresses, Lucas proves surprisingly adept at providing comfort and support. He times contractions, applies pressure to my lower back, and reminds me to breathe through the most intense moments. When Dr. Blake arrives, snow-covered but calm, Lucas follows his instructions competently.

"You're doing beautifully." Dr. Blake checks my progress. "This little one is moving quickly. Won't be long now."

"The nursery isn't finished." The absurd concern escapes between contractions. "The crib isn't assembled."

"I think she'll forgive us." Lucas laughs, pressing a cool cloth to my forehead.

"The birth announcement design isn't finalized." Another ridiculous worry as my body prepares to deliver our child. "And we haven't confirmed her middle name."

"Rose." Lucas's suggestion comes with such certainty that I pause even through the pain. "After the grandmother whose soufflé recipe brought us together."

Tears spring to my eyes at the perfect symmetry of his choice. "Yes. Lily Rose Reid."

Hours compress into a blur of sensation and emotion—pain unlike anything I've experienced, determination beyond what I thought possible, and finally, the transcendent moment when our daughter emerges into Lucas's waiting hands, her angry cry filling the room seconds later.

"She's perfect." Tears stream down his face as he places our daughter on my chest, her tiny body warm and miraculous against my skin. "Absolutely perfect."

Lily Rose Reid enters the world as a snowstorm rages outside—seven pounds of determination and timing entirely her own. With her father's dark hair and what already seems like my stubborn expression, she embodies the unexpected magic that transformed my carefully planned life into something infinitely better.

Dr. Blake handles the necessary medical procedures before leaving us to our first moments as a family, promising to return in the morning to check our progress. As Lucas settles beside us on the bed, one finger trapped in Lily's surprisingly strong grip, the parallel to our beginning strikes me anew.

"One year ago, I arrived here determined to execute the perfect wedding." I trace our daughter's delicate features with wonder. "Instead, I found something far more valuable."

"Imperfect perfection." Lucas completes my thought, pressing a kiss to my temple. "The best kind."

Snow blankets Angel's Peak once again, three months later, transforming the resort into the winter wonderland that first brought us together. Lucas adjusts his camera settings as I stand at the entrance steps, Lily bundled against my chest in a carrier that matches the ivory of my coat.

"A little to the left." He motions with one hand. "I want to capture the exact spot where you fell into my arms."

"And my binder exploded across the snow."

"The universe's most effective introduction." He snaps several photos, moving around to capture different angles. "Though if I'd known what that flustered event planner would become to me, I might have been too intimidated to catch you."

Lily stirs against my chest, her tiny face turning toward her father's voice with the awareness that continues to astonish us both. At three months, she already shows signs of a personality that combines his easy nature and my focused intensity— capable of deep concentration one moment and spontaneous joy the next.

"This will be our tradition." Lucas lowers the camera and moves to join us on the steps. "Annual family photos at the spot where everything began."

"Where disaster became adventure." I lean into him as he wraps an arm around us both. "Where perfection got redefined."

His kiss tastes of possibility and promise—the same flavors that have defined our relationship from its stormy beginning to this moment of quiet wonder. Around us, the resort hums with the activity of another successful event weekend, the business we've built together thriving beyond our initial projections.

But here, on these snow-covered steps where my organized life first tumbled into beautiful chaos, we're simply a family—imperfect, evolving, and exactly as we should be.

"Ready for our next adventure?" Lucas asks, his smile warming me more effectively than any coat.

I look up at the man who taught me to embrace the unexpected, down at the daughter who embodies our unlikely union, and forward to the future we continue to build together.

"Absolutely."

LOVE THE HEAT IN ANGEL'S PEAK?

If you're enjoying all the steamy, small-town instalove stories this mountain town has to offer, you're going to fall hard for *Matched with the Small Town Chef*.

This next swoon-worthy romance serves up spice, sweetness, and a hero who knows exactly what he wants—*her*.

📖 Grab your apron...and your fan. Things are about to get delicious.

⏩ Click here to dive into *Matched with the Small Town Chef!*

SHE CAME TO DESTROY HIS RESTAURANT. HE MADE her hunger for so much more.

Food critic Audrey Tristan—known in the industry as "The Executioner"—arrives in the mountain town of Angel's Peak with one mission: deliver a scathing review that will boost her magazine's circulation. What she doesn't expect is to get trapped in a greenhouse during a sudden storm with a devastatingly attractive stranger whose calloused hands know exactly how to make her body sing.

Hunter Morgan has spent years rebuilding his reputation after his Denver restaurant collapsed in scandal. Now, as head chef of Timberline, he's determined to prove his worth through honest mountain cuisine that honors his grandfather's legacy. The last thing he needs is another critic—especially one whose silver eyes and sharp tongue awaken desires he's kept carefully buried.

When a passionate encounter in his greenhouse leads to explosive nights of surrender and control, Audrey discovers a side of herself she never knew existed. Hunter's commanding presence in the kitchen extends to the bedroom, where he demands her complete submission and gives her pleasure beyond her wildest fantasies.

But when Audrey's true identity is revealed, their scorching connection faces the ultimate test. Can a love built on deception survive the harsh light of truth? Or will the woman known for destroying restaurants find herself destroyed by the one man who made her feel truly alive?

A sizzling enemies-to-lovers romance where a ruthless food critic meets her match in a chef who serves up both culinary perfection and toe-curling dominance.

Tropes in "Stranded with the Chef" 🔥

💀 **Enemies to Lovers** - Food critic vs. chef whose restaurant she's reviewing

🌧️ **Forced Proximity** - Trapped together during mountain storms

🎭 **Secret Identity** - She's undercover as "The Executioner" critic

🔥 **Instalust/Insta-attraction** - Immediate explosive chemistry in the greenhouse

👨‍🍳 **Chef Hero** - Talented, passionate chef rebuilding his reputation

📐 **Career Woman Heroine** - Successful but emotionally guarded food critic

🏔️ **Small Town Romance** - Big city girl falls for mountain town life

🌱 **Found Family** - Heroine finds belonging in tight-knit community

😈 **Dominant/Submissive** - Chef takes control, heroine surrenders

💜 **Second Chance** - Hero rebuilding after professional betrayal

😶 **Secrets & Lies** - Built on professional deception

🏚️ **Emotional Walls** - Both have trust issues from past hurts

🐟 **Fish Out of Water** - City critic adapting to mountain life

🏢 **Workplace Romance** - Professional/personal lines blur

🛖 **Cabin/Shelter Romance** - Intimate encounters in secluded spaces

👵 **Meddling Grandmother** - Hunter's wise grandmother plays matchmaker

Foodie Romance - Cooking as love language and seduction

HEA with Pregnancy - Epilogue includes marriage and baby

High Stakes - Review could make or break his restaurant/town

Multiple Steamy Scenes - Greenhouse, kitchen, cabin encounters

GRAB THE FIRST BOOK IN THE GUARDIAN HOSTAGE RESCUE SPECIALISTS SERIES FOR FREE

https://elliemasters.com/RescuingMelissa

Please consider leaving a review

I hope you enjoyed this book as much as I enjoyed writing it. If you like this book, please leave a review. I love reviews. I love reading your reviews, and they help other readers decide if this book is worth their time and money. I hope you think it is and decide to share this story with others. A sentence is all it takes. Thank you in advance!

Click on the link below to leave your review
Goodreads
Amazon
Bookbub

ELLZ BELLZ

ELLIE'S FACEBOOK READER GROUP

If you are interested in joining the ELLZ BELLZ, Ellie's Facebook reader group, we'd love to have you.

Join Ellie's ELLZ BELLZ.
The ELLZ BELLZ Facebook Reader Group

Sign up for Ellie's Newsletter.
Elliemasters.com/newslettersignup

Also by Ellie Masters

The LIGHTER SIDE

Ellie Masters is the lighter side of the Jet & Ellie Masters writing duo!
You will find Contemporary Romance, Military Romance,
Romantic Suspense, Billionaire Romance, and Rock Star Romance
in Ellie's Works.

YOU CAN FIND ELLIE'S BOOKS HERE:

ELLIEMASTERS.COM/BOOKS

SUGGESTED READING ORDER

START HERE

Rockstar Romance

The Angel Fire Rock Romance Series

EACH BOOK IN THIS SERIES CAN BE READ AS A STANDALONE
AND IS ABOUT A DIFFERENT COUPLE WITH AN HEA. IT IS
RECOMMENDED THEY ARE READ IN ORDER.

Heart's Insanity

Ashes to New

Heart's Desire

Heart's Collide

Hearts Divided

Hearts Entwined

Forest's FALL

Hearts The Last Beat

CONTINUE HERE...

Military Romance

Guardian Hostage Rescue Specialists

Rescuing Melissa

*(*Get a FREE copy of Rescuing Melissa

when you join Ellie's Newsletter*)*

Alpha Team

Rescuing Zoe

Rescuing Moira

Rescuing Eve

Rescuing Lily

Rescuing Jinx

Rescuing Maria

Bravo Team

Rescuing Angie

Rescuing Isabelle

Rescuing Carmen

Rescuing Rosalie

Rescuing Kaye

Cara's Protector

Rescuing Barbi

Charlie Team

Rescuing Rebel

Rescuing Stitch

Rescuing Mia

Jenna's Protector

Rescuing Sophia

By Jet & Ellie Masters

Ellie Masters writing as L.A. Warren

Vendel Rising: a Science Fiction Serialized Novel

If you enjoyed this book by Ellie Masters, the LIGHTER SIDE of the Jet & Ellie writing duo, and aren't afraid of edgier writing, you might enjoy reading BDSM themed books written by Jet, the DARKER SIDE of the Masters' Writing Team.

The DARKER SIDE

Jet Masters is the darker side of the Jet & Ellie writing duo!

Romantic Suspense

Changing Roles Series:

THIS SERIES MUST BE READ IN ORDER.

Command Me

Control Me

Collar Me

Embracing FATE

Seizing FATE

Accepting FATE

HOT READS

A STANDALONE NOVEL.

Down the Rabbit Hole

Light BDSM Romance
The Ties that Bind

EACH BOOK IN THIS SERIES CAN BE READ AS A STANDALONE AND IS ABOUT A DIFFERENT COUPLE WITH AN HEA.

Alexa

Penny

Michelle

Ivy

HOT READS

Becoming His Series

THIS SERIES MUST BE READ IN ORDER.

The Ballet

Learning to Breathe

Becoming His

Dark Captive Romance

A STANDALONE NOVEL.

She's MINE

Books by Jet Masters

If you enjoyed this book by Ellie Masters, the LIGHTER SIDE of the Jet & Ellie writing duo, and aren't afraid of edgier writing, you might enjoy reading BDSM themed books written by Jet, the DARKER SIDE of the Masters' Writing Team.

The DARKER SIDE
Jet Masters is the darker side of the Jet & Ellie writing duo!

Romantic Suspense
Changing Roles Series:
THIS SERIES MUST BE READ IN ORDER.
Command Me
Control Me
Collar Me
Embracing FATE
Seizing FATE
Accepting FATE

HOT READS

A STANDALONE NOVEL.
Down the Rabbit Hole

Light BDSM Romance
The Ties that Bind

EACH BOOK IN THIS SERIES CAN BE READ AS A
STANDALONE AND IS ABOUT A DIFFERENT COUPLE
WITH AN HEA.

Alexa
Penny
Michelle
Ivy

HOT READS
Becoming His Series

THIS SERIES MUST BE READ IN ORDER.
The Ballet
Learning to Breathe
Becoming His

Dark Captive Romance

A STANDALONE NOVEL.
She's MINE

ABOUT THE AUTHOR

Ellie Masters is a USA Today Bestselling author and Amazon Top 15 Author who writes Angsty, Steamy, Heart-Stopping, Pulse-Pounding, Can't-Stop-Reading Romantic Suspense. In addition, she's a wife, military mom, doctor, and retired Colonel. She writes romantic suspense filled with all your sexy, swoon-worthy alpha men. Her writing will tug at your heart-strings and leave your heart racing.

Born in the South, raised under the Hawaiian sun, Ellie has traveled the globe while in service to her country. The love of her life, her amazing husband, is her number one fan and biggest supporter. And yes! He's read every word she's written.

She has lived all over the United States—east, west, north, south and central—but grew up under the Hawaiian sun. She's also been privileged to have lived overseas, experiencing other cultures and making lifelong friends. Now, Ellie is proud to call herself a Southern transplant, learning to say y'all and "bless her heart" with the best of them.

Ellie's favorite way to spend an evening is curled up on a couch, laptop in place, watching a fire, drinking a good wine, and bringing forth all the characters from her mind to the page and hopefully into the hearts of her readers.

FOR MORE INFORMATION
elliemasters.com

facebook.com/elliemastersromance

x.com/Ellie__Masters

instagram.com/ellie_masters

bookbub.com/authors/ellie-masters

goodreads.com/Ellie_Masters

CONNECT WITH ELLIE MASTERS

Website:
elliemasters.com
Purchase Direct:
elliemasters.com/shopify
Amazon Author Page:
elliemasters.com/amazon
Facebook:
elliemasters.com/Facebook
Goodreads:
elliemasters.com/Goodreads
Bookbub:
elliemasters.com/Bookbub
Instagram:
elliemasters.com/Instagram

Final Thoughts

I hope you enjoyed this book as much as I enjoyed writing it. If you enjoyed reading this story, please consider leaving a review on Amazon and Goodreads, and please let other people know. A sentence is all it takes. Friend recommendations are the strongest catalyst for readers' purchase decisions! And I'd love to be able to continue bringing the characters and stories from My-Mind-to-the-Page.

Second, call or e-mail a friend and tell them about this book. If you really want them to read it, gift it to them. If you prefer digital friends, please use the "Recommend" feature of Goodreads to spread the word.

Or visit my blog https://elliemasters.com, where you can find out more about my writing process and personal life.

Come visit The EDGE: Dark Discussions where we'll have a chance to talk about my works, their creation, and maybe what the future has in store for my writing.

Facebook Reader Group: Ellz Bellz

Thank you so much for your support!

Love,

Ellie

DEDICATION

This book is dedicated to you, my reader. Thank you for spending a few hours of your time with me. I wouldn't be able to write without you to cheer me on. Your wonderful words, your support, and your willingness to join me on this journey is a gift beyond measure.

Whether this is the first book of mine you've read, or if you've been with me since the very beginning, thank you for believing in me as I bring these characters 'from my mind to the page and into your hearts.'

Love,
Ellie

THE END

Printed in Dunstable, United Kingdom